TROUBLE ON A COUNTRY LANE

Isabella Bassett

CONTENTS

CHAPTER 1

England, 1925

Father's dogs sensed my mother's approach first.

Until that moment, the collection of misfits and mutts had lounged on the Aubusson carpets lining the drawing room's floors, rubbing their flea-ridden backs against the thick wool pile, in a nonchalant disregard for propriety. But presently, they sprang for the double doors, their claws failing to afford them any grip on the polished hardwood floors, and skidding to a stop, lined up like soldiers in order of height, awaiting her arrival.

For those in doubt of the dogs' competence, a voice piercing the air of the hallway beyond the double doors with the power of a locomotive whistle—calling on various servants to join her—heralded my mother's impending approach.

The grand doors swung open, and my mother

breezed in, trailed by her retinue of a private secretary, an assistant to the private secretary, the butler, a pair of footmen and a quartet of pageboys.

Unlike most families of our milieu, my mother continued to employ an unabridged set of servants. Her extravagant dowry, being one of the notorious 'dollar princesses', had guaranteed that she could not only refurbish the family's medieval castle with the latest conveniences of indoor plumbing, but also retain all her domestics—both rarities among the impoverished aristocrats of the land after the Great War.

She had yet to notice my presence in the room. Sitting in a wing chair in an alcove by the bow window, I watched her from the relative seclusion of my seat as she tried to maneuver the couch and sit down. The house cat, a stray tabby that had arrived one day and refused to leave, spared her a cross-eyed glance, but did not budge from her spot on the couch.

The seat of contention happened to be right under the outsized Sargent portrait of my mother —confident forward stance, smirk, gazing directly at the viewer—painted on the occasion of her debut in Boston. My mother loved sitting under the portrait. It served the twofold purpose of showcasing to hapless visitors her social stature, as evidenced by having been painted by the great artist, and tacitly imparting the fact that she had lost none of her youth and radiant beauty since the portrait was painted, despite having four grown children. One had to concede that the former assured the admiration of male visitors, while the latter greatly intimidated female ones.

Perhaps sensing that this was the spot where the most important family member sat, the cat found it equally attractive, and strived to usurp it from my mother on any occasion.

After a few tense moments of a silent battle of wills, my mother relented and picked another place to sit.

Observing the incident, I knew there was a lesson for us all in what had just transpired, but my musings were cut short by my mother, who had spotted me at that very moment.

"Caroline!" she exclaimed in her measured, cultured voice. "What are you doing, hiding there?"

I was not hiding. I had been going through the day's correspondence. Although I had been back in England less than a week, invitations to various parties, dances and soirees had begun pouring in. Chums like Edwina Thomson-Brown, Lilibeth Galardsel, and Clementine Westley expressed profusely their desire to see me again. But there was only one invitation that had attracted my attention.

My mother beckoned me towards her with an elegant hand, discreetly bedecked in a few priceless family jewels that were rumored to be the envy of Queen Mary. Though as fond of jewelry as the Queen, my mother thankfully showed more restraint when it came to adornments.

Although the daughter of a Boston businessman, my mother did not let the fact that she had not been born into the aristocracy trouble her. In fact, she believed that the Boston Brahmin class in which she was born was much more exclusive. As she was fond of saying, one could not buy their way into a Boston Brahmin family. This implied that while places in the penurious British aristocracy could easily be obtained through the simple transaction of a marriage, as her own matrimonial merger attested, Boston Brahmins had enough money to not be swayed by such base needs in their nuptial decisions. Assured of her superiority of birth, she carried herself accordingly.

"Don't slouch," she admonished as she surveyed my progress through the cavernous room towards her. "If you only chose to make the best of your looks," she continued, "you would not now find yourself in this unhappy situation." She waved an embellished hand to encompass all my purported troubles.

As anyone familiar with my mother would immediately deduce, she was referring to my unmarried status at the age of twenty-five.

For the record, my slouching—which I wasn't —had nothing to do with my lack of marital bliss.

Neither did my looks. I knew for a fact that my fair hair, cropped in the latest style, clear complexion, dazzling smile and slim figure were well regarded in society. I held no false, self-deprecating views about my attractiveness.

What held me back from the latest score of proposals was my considerable wealth. A large sum of money had been settled on my name when I'd come of age, and I was weary of giving control of it to just any unworthy young man who came along.

Dwelling on the topic of marriage, my thoughts drifted back to the envelope at the top of the pile I held in my hand. Its gilded paper had not escaped my mother's notice, who was eyeing it suspiciously.

"Is that the engagement party invitation from Lord and Lady Haswell?" she inquired rhetorically, between rattling off correspondence replies and household directions to the retinue surrounding her. Pageboys punctuated our discourse by running out of the room at regular intervals.

"It is," I said, running my fingers nervously over the embossed frills of the linen paper. I had to be prudent in my next steps. "And I'd very much like to attend," I said in a diffident voice.

The invitation had arrived this morning. It was for the impending engagement of Lord Haswell's eldest son, Leopold, to a wealthy American named Daphne Carter. Although currently using the courtesy title of Viscount Otley, Leopold was in line to be the seventh Earl of Haswell. But a mere title had not been sufficient to persuade any eligible girl on this side of the pond to enter into a union with him, so it seemed the Haswells had trawled foreign shores for a bride. I shuddered at the thought of having to spend one's life with such a bore as Leopold.

But it was not lowbrow curiosity of glimpsing the American who was about to venture into a union none of us had dared, which drew me to the engagement party. (Though I had to admit it presented a certain attraction). Nor was my desire to attend entirely prompted by the wish to quit the family abode—and my mother's crosshairs —to which I had drifted reluctantly after the latest incident with Uncle Albert. And although attending the engagement party, which happened to be held at Lord Haswell's summer house in Kent, would allow me to check on Uncle Albert's current predicament, I had to admit that familial duty was also not the reason why I was desirous of partaking in this particular gathering.

The strongest draw for me to the engagement party was the assured attendance of James— fourth son of Lord Haswell and Leopold's younger brother.

James had been my late brother Charles' closest friend. They had gone to university, and then to the front, together. My brother hadn't returned.

Only a few years older than me, I had to admit I'd had a schoolgirl crush on James for as long as I could remember, and the engagement party invitation had brought those thoughts to the fore.

As the fourth son of an Earl, James was still unmarried, and had little prospect of doing so, unless he married a wealthy wife. And while I was more than willing to consider such an arrangement, he had never asked. Was a modern woman allowed to propose marriage? I wondered for a moment. Maybe I should. Or was I afraid of rejection? Was I more comfortable living with the dream of what could be?

I shook my head and resolved to make my intentions towards James very clear at the engagement party.

"Well, put all such nonsense out of your mind," my mother's voice cut into my musings, as she paused between dictating a letter to her secretary to chide me, and I wondered for a moment if I had spoken my thoughts aloud.

"Sorry, what nonsense?" I asked, perturbed.

"Going to Leopold's engagement party, of course. There is little for you there. You had your chance of marrying him several times." She gave me a meaningful look and now focused her attention on the rest of the letters in my hand. "You had much better to go to Edwina Thomson-Brown's soiree. I'm sure her cousin Alistair will be in attendance."

I shuddered once again. There was nothing wrong with Edwina Thomson-Brown and her ability to throw a jolly good party. In fact, she was one of my good chums. But even if the presence of her cousin Alistair was not enough to deter any sprightly young maiden from attending, it was the prospect of the indisputable absence of James from said soiree that dissuaded me from patronizing the bash in question.

But before I could voice my objection, something in the garden caught my mother's attention.

"What is that man doing here again?" she asked, and glided to the French doors overlooking the gardens. "It's the third time this week!"

CHAPTER 2

The dogs pushed past my mother—eliciting a cry of outrage from her—and jumped out of the French doors to run and greet the vicar who had just joined my father in the garden.

Mother eyed the pair for a long moment. She'd developed a nascent dislike for the vicar.

Upon returning to the home pile, I'd learned that our local vicar, Rev. Bamford, and my father had not long ago become much closer acquaintances, drawn together by a newly discovered mutual interest in Thomas Becket. My mother abhorred the idea that the two men in her life she had commanded so completely until recently had now an interest that excluded her.

My mother viewed this as a change of allegiance on the part of the vicar and felt double-crossed by him.

Having her momentarily distracted, I pressed my case. "But what about Uncle Albert?" I said, trying a new angle. "Should I not pay a visit to him at the sanatorium? He's not far from the Haswells.

Perhaps he has some letters he needs me to write."

While I was officially still my uncle's private secretary, my uncle was sequestered in a place where he didn't require my services for the foreseeable future.

"Don't mention your Uncle Albert in my presence," she said haughtily, still gazing at the men through the open garden doors. I wondered what the aged relation had done to upset her. "He has a lot to answer for," she said, turning away from the gardens and walking back to the sofa. "All those dead bodies you're constantly running into."

"It's not by his design," I countered politely.

My mother looked unconvinced. Sitting back down, she resumed holding her court.

Perhaps this was not a good time to remind her that the idea to pack me off to be Uncle Albert's secretary had been hers. But although I had accepted the assignment somewhat unwillingly, I had grown to like working for my uncle since then. There was a certain refreshing exhilaration in the guarantee that wherever he was, trouble was always near.

I decided to keep all of these thoughts to myself.

Having anticipated just such a resistance from my mother, I had an alternate plan. One did not spend twenty-odd years in the same house as mother, without developing some war tactics.

"I could accompany the vicar to Canterbury,"

I suggested. "You know how he is. He's bound to leave the most important items on the train. Is it not better that I accompany him to his meeting with the Archbishop and make certain he and his wares arrive safely?"

She paused just long enough before answering to give to the uninitiated the impression that she was considering my suggestion.

"Yes, it's foolish of your father to trust the vicar so implicitly. He does tend to drop things…" she trailed off.

Although my proposal was sound, I knew she resisted accepting it because the suggestion had not sprung from her. And yet, I could see her being torn between not letting me get my way and safeguarding the family's treasures that the vicar would soon be spiriting off to Canterbury.

Upon a recent visit to the house, the vicar had discovered a dusty tapestry hanging in a forgotten tower depicting a hunt, which he had become convinced was an allegory for Thomas Becket's life and martyrdom. In addition to the tapestry, he had gathered, with the help of my father, some supporting materials for his theory, such as a terribly rare illuminated text by monks of the Arbroath Abbey in Scotland, and a reliquary containing drops of Thomas Becket's blood adorned with motifs similar to ones found on the tapestry.

The vicar had gathered all these items and

was preparing a showstopper of sorts with which to dazzle the Archbishop of Canterbury. The Archbishop, concerned with dwindling attendance, had convened a colloquium in Canterbury in a few days' time, whereby country vicars were invited to bring forth and exhibit treasures from their parishes which could then be used to impress their parishioners and thus bolster flailing numbers.

The vicar had got it into his mind that these Thomas Becket trinkets would restore him to the Archbishop's favor.

My heart went out to Rev. Bamford as I watched him trip around the garden. It was said, by gossips in the back pews during service on Sundays, that at one point, the vicar had had a promising career ahead of him. His full head of hair, the gossips went on, had predicted a stellar rise in the church. But that had been before my mother had married my father. Since her arrival, he had gone bald and his career had gone the way of his hair. He now lived in a state of perpetual agitation and was prone to dropping things in my mother's presence.

"Darling," my mother said in a voice that made it clear I was not her darling at the moment, "I know perfectly well what you are doing. And after conveying the vicar, you'll want to pop off to the engagement party."

The look my mother gave me suggested that underestimating her had been my first tactical mistake. *So much for my plan,* I sighed internally.

"Caroline, darling," she continued, "I've met the people who are going to be marrying into Lord Haswell's family. They are quite the wrong sort. The most vile American upstarts." That was rich coming from a 'dollar princess' I thought. But the duplicity was completely lost on my mother. She sat straight-backed, slightly to the side of her Sargent portrait, gazing haughtily in the distance, as though foraging in the rich fauna of jibes Brits reserved for Americans, for an additional insult to throw at them. "They are from New York, for goodness' sake!" she exclaimed at last, having finally latched onto a juicy one. "They are not even from Boston!" She might as well have added that they did not have portraits by Sargent hanging in their drawing rooms. "Didn't even know who Sargent was!" she scoffed, affirming my sentiment.

Upon my return home, my mother had not spared me the account of the visit of the Haswells and their future in-laws. She was furious the Haswells had had the audacity to presume that my mother would enjoy the company of such uncouth upstarts just because they were Americans. She had lamented the insult of springing them up on her unwarned.

She now threw me a look that said her argument against attending the engagement party was complete and irrefutable. I relented for the time being.

Sensing my vulnerability, my mother used the opportunity to latch onto her favorite topic—a triptych of woe worthy of any church altar—of how I had ruined my chances of securing a good marriage. The central theme comprised of how I'd refused every eligible bachelor, and was buttressed on each side by the imprudence of attending a London typing school on a lark, and the recently acquired tendency of engaging in ruinous escapades of murder and mayhem.

The theme was my ever-present companion, and I listened to my mother without malice. One of my mother's greatest sources of disappointment was her immediate family. While she could corral her servants with ease, her efforts were forever thwarted by her nearest relations.

"Your shenanigans in London and refusal to marry are a constant source of trepidation for me," she bemoaned with what I knew was false dejection.

I did not reply, but I took comfort in the knowledge that I was not the only family member who tarnished the family's image, at least according to my mother.

"Your Uncle Albert is a loose cannon," she continued with a speech I had heard many times. "Your father's aunts disgrace themselves with their interest in the occult and the incessant deathly prediction of one family member or other. Your brother Edward is most likely drinking himself into oblivion at his London club. I cannot fathom why. I would be more than happy to be inheriting a title." She looked at her secretary, who nodded her agreement on the matter. "At least your sister Theodora made a good match," she said with a sigh.

What my mother's sigh concealed was that Theodora's fault was that she was not pretty enough. And though that was something my sister could not help, it was a flaw my mother could not overlook.

In fact, the only one of her children who had not disappointed her in some way was my brother Charles, but he was dead.

"And now, I worry about your father," she said, directing her gaze towards the gardens again, though the men seemed to have walked out of view. "Carrying on with the vicar like that, encouraging him to have ideas above his station and persuading him to go to Canterbury. What do they find so interesting to talk about, locked up in the library or his office, all day?"

Perhaps the greatest source of anxiety for my mother was my father and his failure to live up to what she thought was the full potential of his station in life. She would have preferred someone more ambitious, taller, slimmer, an all-round less awkward chap. But alas, as the bearer of the family title, she was stuck with him.

I stood there, gripped by melancholy,

wondering if I'd ever make it to the party, when the double doors crashed open.

CHAPTER 3

"It's missing!" my father exclaimed and stumbled in as the doors banged open. He was clearly in distress. The dogs, excited by the commotion, ran back into the room after my father, their claws clicking on the floor, and gathered around him with wagging tails.

My mother did a double take. I understood her confusion. Just moments ago, my father had been out in the garden with the vicar. Why was he now entering the drawing room through the hallway?

"What is missing, my dearest?" she turned to my father with a chilly voice that belied her term of endearment. My father was in the habit of misplacing things.

"My cross!" my father exclaimed, his eyes darting over the tables in the drawing room, as though he hoped he'd left the missing cross on one of their surfaces.

"Which cross?" she asked, slightly testily.

"The Order of the Conqueror's Companions cross!" he answered, exasperated. But it was a fair question. In a house, where certain parts dated from the 12th century, there were many crosses to be mislaid.

"Oh!" I could see apprehension transform my mother's beautiful mask.

Despite their superficial disagreements, if there was one thing that united my parents, it was their sense of superiority over their peers. My mother was a member of the Boston Brahmins. My father was a member of the Order of the Conqueror's Companions.

My father's own aforementioned interest in Thomas Becket stemmed from the fact that he and the saint both descended from the most trusted knights of William the Conqueror. This quirk of history afforded my father a place in the Order of the Conqueror's Companions, a quasi-secret society, whose secrecy was due more to its exclusivity than to any concerted effort on the part of its members to keep it secret.

The order comprised the fifteen direct male descendants of the knights who fought alongside Duke William at the Battle of Hastings and thus had only fifteen members at a time. Thomas Becket, a second generation descendent of a family that fought alongside William, was the spiritual founding member of the Order and its patron saint.

Though there were undoubtedly more knights who took part in the infamous battle, the names of only fifteen knights were mentioned in reliable sources, much to our current King's chagrin. The King, although claiming to be a descendent of William the Conqueror, was much more closely related to Germanic royal houses than the Normans.

It was something of a favorite quip among the members of the Order of the Conqueror's Companions, that the royal family, having been excluded from the Order a few centuries ago, had been forced to create the Order of the Garter, and modeled it after the Conqueror's Companions.

Of all my father's endeavors, the Order was one that my mother supported most whole-heartedly. She understood its importance to my father's elevated standing in society. It separated him from all the other run-of-the-mill Earls that the countryside was littered with.

"I can't go to the Order's conclave without my cross," my father moaned, and sat heavily in the nearest armchair. The dogs convened around him like a knight's counsel.

All those gathered in the drawing room, and by now we were joined by the housekeeper and the parlormaid, comprehended the gravity of the situation. In addition to being a direct descendant of one of the fifteen knights, each Order member had to bring along five attributes to every meeting to confirm his worthiness of remaining a member of the Order: cape, cross, sword, shield and reins.

The absence of any one of the attributes would

jeopardize the member's standing in the Order and threaten him with excommunication.

One of my father's favorite pastimes was showing off his regalia to visitors and then promptly mislaying them, which guaranteed that any one of these five articles was missing at any one time. The months prior to the annual conclave were distinguished by furious searches across the house for said articles.

"Where did you see it last?" my mother asked, concerned.

"Well, I was about to show it to the vicar..." my father answered, waving a hand vaguely towards his study.

"Yes, but when did you actually see your cross?" my mother pressed.

My father's brow furrowed, and he enumerated silently something on the fingers of his hand. "When I was showing it to the Americans," he finally announced.

"When Lord Haswell and his family came to visit?" I asked, and threw my mother a furtive glance.

My father nodded in confirmation.

"And you haven't seen it after?" I asked.

He shook his head.

I watched as comprehension dawned on my mother's face. "You don't think..." She did not complete her thought. "It's just too distressing that someone would stoop so low..."

"What are you suggesting, mother?" I asked, intrigued. "Do you think the American guests could have taken it?"

I could see her reluctance to throw such a vile accusation at the feet of one of her compatriots, no matter how uncouth they were.

"No, I wouldn't think so," my father interjected. "They didn't strike me as the type of people who appreciate the finer nuances of British history." He paused to consider the significance of this. "I would not put it past Lord Haswell, however," he continued.

"What?" I said, astonished. "You think Lord Haswell is behind this?"

The expression on my mother's face, however, revealed that her thoughts had been flowing in line with my father's.

"He'd do anything to discredit my membership in the Order," my father said. "Lord Haswell has been looking for years for an excuse to get me excommunicated from the Order, to further his own political career. The swine," he added under his breath. "Thinks he's better than me simply because his Norman ancestor happens to be embroidered one additional time on the Bayeux Tapestry." My father glared in the middle distance at the injustice of fate.

"I should not wonder...now that they find themselves in such dire financial difficulties..." my mother said, adding fuel to my father's argument.

"They are?" I asked. Clearly, I had missed a lot while being away from home.

"Yes," my father said, perking up. "Lord Haswell has accumulated crippling debts due to some dubious investments in South America."

"Why do you think they are in a hurry to marry off someone as handsome as Leopold to a rich American?" my mother added.

My mother and I had divergent criteria for attractiveness. Titles, for my mother, always improved one's looks.

My father shifted uncomfortably at the unintended—or was it?—slight regarding the nature of Anglo-American marriages.

"They are even considering selling their Kentish estate to the Americans to raise more money," she added, visibly distressed by the possibility of a peer having to part with one of his properties.

My mother's scathing assessment of the Haswells' future in-laws, coupled with Lord Haswell's money troubles, piqued my interest. "Who is this American?" I asked.

"A Mr. Carter," said my father.

"A New York businessman of uncertain origins," my mother added with distaste. "Quite wealthy, by all accounts. He's looking to enter politics, either to further his business affairs or to satisfy some need for fulfillment. He bored us quite at length about it during dinner. The crux of it is that he's buying his way into the British aristocracy to raise his profile back in America."

The Haswells and their future American in-laws were abused for a few more minutes. But presently, Father's heavy sigh returned everyone's attention to the problem at hand. "What am I to do about my cross?"

"Has no one else been in your study since their visit?" I asked.

My father shook his head and let his chin fall on his chest.

That was all the testimony my mother required to spring into action. Footmen and pageboys spread out through the house to search for the cross. The secretary was tasked with compiling a list of the best jewelers in London for the purpose of having a replica made in time for the conclave. The butler was sent to telephone the pre-eminent scholars on Norman Britain from Oxford and Cambridge with the aim of locating a hetero forgotten cross.

When all the staff had withdrawn, and only the family circle remained, my mother leaned back into the sofa and descended into silence. She motioned that I should not leave the room quite yet. Observing her closely, I could see schemes flash across her face. A slight spasm accompanied the dismissal of each one in turn. At last, a small smile spread across her face.

"Where is the vicar now?" my mother asked.

"In the library, looking for more things to show the Archbishop..." my father said.

Speaking of the devil, as it were, through the open doors, with the corner of my eye, I spied the vicar slinking along the walls, trying to blend with the darker corners of the hallway.

Had the vicar asked my advice—assuming he desired to withdraw from the house undetected by Mother—I could have imparted a few tricks, such as using Father's study to exit through the back gardens. The monstrous topiary of a swan created a flawless blind-spot for entering and exiting the house through that room.

As it was, my mother had no trouble spotting him among the shadows thrown by the suits of armor.

"Ah, vicar! There you are!" she cried in a voice that left the hearer in no doubt that he was being summoned. "I found the perfect solution to your Canterbury conundrum."

The vicar displayed a countenance that gave the onlooker to understand that he had up to presently not been aware of such a conundrum, but the expression quickly dissolved into an obliging mask, and he presented himself to Mother, awaiting her instructions.

"I am sure you would be most delighted to learn that Caroline has volunteered to convey you to Canterbury."

He dropped a few of the items he was cradling, underlying my mother's belief that he needed a chaperone.

I lifted an eyebrow in surprise. The vicar would say that Providence had intervened.

CHAPTER 4

While the footmen were packing my shiny two-seater roadster for our trip with the vicar, my thoughts drifted back to the drawing room conversation of the previous day.

My mother's suggestion that I should go to Canterbury, and the implied understanding that I could attend the engagement party, had not been a sign of capitulation on her part.

"Caroline," she had turned to me. "It's time you employ those purported skills of yours for the good of the family. Your attendance at the Haswell engagement party should give you ample opportunity to search for the cross."

I had feigned outrage at my mother's suggestion that I should act like a common criminal. She received my objections in the same spirit in which they were given, and completely dismissed them.

The truth was, however, that my mother was quite right in her estimations of my penchant for stratagems. I was not only known as a champion scavenger hunt competitor among my chums in

London, but I had also attended a finishing school in Switzerland which had prepared me, unwittingly, for just such underhand practices.

The headmistress, Frau Baumgartnerhoff, recently divorced and eternally embittered, had given her charges all the tools necessary for a bit of domestic subterfuge. She had intended for these skills to be used to uncover unsavory behaviors of husbands, but I'd found that these same competences could just as easily be employed in recovering missing artifacts or sussing out murderers.

Assured of the success of at least one of the schemes she had put in motion, my mother had soon put the affair of the Order cross out of her mind.

But I had remained curious to know my father's feelings on the matter. And I'd found him sitting on a stone bench, hidden behind the tall boxwood walls of the topiary garden, staring into space.

"I would not mind it so much," he'd said without preamble, as I took a seat next to him. "But your mother would be so terribly upset if I lost my spot in the Order."

"Do you think it's possible that Lord Haswell's American, Mr. Carter, took it?" I asked.

"Oh, no. I'm quite confident in my estimation of him. He would not be interested in such things," he said, shaking his head. "No, it's an inside job."

I leaped slightly off the stone surface, as though

zapped by a frayed electric cable. Did my father suspect someone other than Lord Haswell?

"Do you mean one of the staff?" I asked, incredulous.

"Absolutely not," my father said categorically. "What would they want with such a thing?"

While my father valued the cross only for its historical significance and the membership it afforded him in the Order, the cross had an intrinsic worth far beyond the historical. It was fashioned out of solid gold, with a diamond centerpiece encircled with sapphires. The stones alone would be quite valuable to a working person. They would probably set them up for a few years.

"Risk their position and good name for a trinket that's only of any use to fifteen people in the Empire?" he continued. "No, I don't for a moment suspect any of the household staff."

My father was probably right. Most of our staff had been with us for many years. And while the cross was valuable, it was by far not the most precious item in the house. The staff would have had plenty of time and opportunity to help themselves to other costly items that would not be so readily missed, if that had been their inclination.

"So why suspect an inside job?" I asked.

"One of our class, I mean to say. So few people know about the Order, and who else would desire such a thing?"

"What about the vicar?" I suggested. "He does have a keen interest in the Norman period and has been visiting the house quite often."

My father considered the possibility and shook his head. "Our vicar is no thief. He's far more stimulated by moth-eaten tapestries and moldy books than shiny metal."

"It could be a ruse on his part?" I suggested.

"No, not our vicar. His failures in this life have sharpened his attachment to the other-worldly. If he were an ambitious man, he would have left this parish long ago. Your mother means well, but she hardly lets anyone shine brighter than herself. The vicar is a humble man. He has contented himself with the simpler pleasures in life. The cross, being of non-ecclesiastical nature, is of no appeal to him."

"So you're quite set on Lord Haswell as the culprit?" I asked.

He nodded. "Lord Haswell is a scoundrel. You know, he was quite uncharitable back in the day when I married your mother. I could not have cared one iota how much fortune she brought with her, though that seemed to be important to my parents...No, your mother's beauty was simply divine. Still is." A misty look clouded his eyes. I was happy to see that even after all the years of being henpecked, my father still found something to admire about my mother. "Lord Haswell made all sorts of jokes at my expense at the time. Now he'll have to eat his hat, and swallow the buckle whole, courting the wealthy American in that unseemly fashion, just for his money."

"But why would Lord Haswell take your cross now?" I asked, not seeing the connection.

"To elevate his own acclaim by diminishing mine," he said. "Petty men are prone to do that, especially when they find themselves in difficult circumstances."

I'd sat next to my father in companionable silence for a while and I marveled at how, in the seclusion of the garden, away from my mother's omnipotent gazes and ever-present intrigues, my father was free to be calm and logical.

I now returned my attention to the vicar. He was pacing nervously and noisily on the gravel driveway, balancing various packages in his arms with care, awaiting our departure. Every so often, he would put the packages down, lift his hat and wipe off the perspiration accumulated under it. I wondered whether his anxiety was due to his natural disposition or to the fact that I was to be driving.

"If I may, Lady Caroline," a voice floated across the driveway. It was Cuthbert, our butler. He approached the car unhurriedly. "The Ladies Mable, Mavis and Myrtle, have telephoned. They have tasked me with relaying a message to you."

My three paternal aunts were always very caring. Fate had been unkind to them, supplying them with husbands to rob them of their wealth, but their good manners remained intact. They were partial to sending messages of encouragement to family members, especially when said members were due to set off on voyages and excursions.

"Is it from beyond?" I asked.

"It would appear so," he affirmed. Regrettably, of late, their messages had been guided by forces encountered in spiritual seances. "Shall I read it?"

I nodded.

He unfolded a crisp piece of paper and cleared his throat. "Death awaits at the end. All roads lead to death. At the end of life is death. The road of life ends with death. The road of life is never straight, and death awaits one at the end." He looked up from his paper. "Your Aunts could not agree on which declaration most accurately summarized the sentiment of the spirit that had delivered it, but seemed to settle on the last one as the most lyrical." He folded the paper. "I wish you a pleasant journey." He bowed slightly and withdrew.

Cuthbert had delivered the message without batting an eyelash, as it were. He was quite used to such pronouncements of doom being conveyed over the telephone line on a regular basis. But it would appear that the vicar, though a constant companion of death in the parish, was unaccustomed to such news. He had dropped all his amulets and books, and was now in the process of gathering them.

"Pay no attention to my aunts," I said, as I dusted off one of his brown paper packages and handed it to him. "They are fond of such prophecies. With as large a family tree as ours, there is always bound to be someone falling permanently off a branch. But be assured that my aunts usually pin the prediction on the wrong person."

Apparently that had not appeased the vicar because he was quite ashen-faced as he got into the car. Shrugging, I hoped the bracing summer breeze would dislodge any fanciful ideas from his head and roared off.

CHAPTER 5

Nervous about losing his Homburg hat to the wind, the vicar had taken it off a while back. The wind now flapped through his anemic hair, and I was worried, in turn, that it would blow off the few tresses he had left.

"It was commendable of your mother to suggest this road trip," the vicar said, overcoming his agitation. My gaze traveled to his hands. They lay on either side of the boxes in his lap and were anchored—with a white-knuckled grip—to the umbrella placed across his knees, forming a sort of wall around his tower of brown-papered earthly delights.

In addition to the hat, the vicar's lap was piled high with all the attributes he was carrying to Canterbury, which in the day preceding our departure had inexplicably grown, and now included various brown paper packages of odd shapes and sizes. But pride of place was still the rolled up tapestry, which hit my elbow every time I shifted gears.

As I hugged another corner, the vicar clutched his umbrella like a drowning man holding on to the proverbial straw. But he needn't have worried. I had perfected my automobile handling in Frau Baumgartnerhoff's finishing school along the hairpin turns of Swiss Alpine roads.

I wondered if the vicar's evident anxiety was perhaps heightened by my aunts' predictions. But the glory of the English countryside in August soon enchanted us.

We drove down quiet country lanes, making our way to Kent. Birds fleeted between the hedgerows. Here and there, trees leaned over the lanes creating green tunnels of canopy. The sun dappled our faces as we drove under their shimmering leaves. Tidy ancient villages and seas of golden fields took turns delighting us. The ripe wheat swayed gently in the warm summer breeze as we drove on. Cattle grazed in pastures. White sheep dotted the green meadows. Poppies blazed in the tall summer grass. Tiny black dots moved rhythmically near tall haystacks—farmers making hay on this sunny day.

The pastoral vista seemed to lift the vicar's spirit, and his grip on the black umbrella relaxed.

Past London, the vicar's mood improved enough to allow him to remind me that we were on the same road as Chaucer, making a modern day pilgrimage to the great Cathedral City. "The good Lord himself would not object to such a trip," the vicar quipped. *"And all the veins are bathed in liquor of such power, as brings about the engendering of the flower*," he quoted from Chaucer. "Oh, one wishes Chaucer had traveled in August so he could have described the beauty of the English countryside in summer. The fecund land, heavy with sweet juices, ripe for the picking by the strong, muscular hand of the farmer..."

The vicar cleared his throat.

But he was right. Something about nature's glory in summer indeed turned one's mind to fecundity and love. My own thoughts had been pleasantly occupied with notions of James and the fact that I was soon to see him.

I was looking forward to spending time in James' company, away from the rigors of secretarial work. And I hoped that the engagement party would set his own thoughts on the course of wooing.

As I drove down the tranquil roads, I considered that it seemed as though the Fates themselves had cleared my way to James. First, I'd learned that Lady Morton's repugnant Cecil was recently engaged, and now the same fate was soon to befall on Leopold. It was as though all the odious bachelors my mother had been endeavoring to align me with were falling by the side, and my road to James was cleared of obstacles.

Thus, with lifted spirits, I looked forward to reaching Resington Hall, the scene of the engagement party. Situated in the Kent Downs, not far from Canterbury, Resington Hall had been the summer residence of the Haswell family since time immemorial. My late brother Charles had spent many summer holidays there, visiting James.

"...and of course the Battle of Hastings took place not far from here, if one were to turn towards the sea..." the vicar was saying. I realized with a start that he must have been talking for a while. I was about to resume ignoring him when he said, "A battle so dear to your own family. Your father informs me, most regrettably, that the cross of the Order of the Conqueror's Companions appears to have gone missing."

I turned sharply to him, and almost drove the car off the road. Regaining my composure, I nodded stiffly and wondered why my father had confided in the vicar. I was positive my mother would not want the news of the missing cross widely known. It would spell disaster for my father's standing in society. At least, according to her.

For a moment I wondered if I should ask him if he knew something about its disappearance, but decided to change the topic. "Where are you staying in Canterbury?" I asked, as we were soon to reach the crossroad for Canterbury. I planned to deposit him and his packages in Canterbury and then continue to Resington Hall.

"Oh, Lady Haswell has been kind enough to extend the invitation to me as well," the vicar said.

"That's terribly kind of her, indeed," I said. The vicar was not known for being the life of the party, as it were, and I wondered what had prompted the lady of the house to invite the vicar.

"Not at all," he said. "My mother and Lady Haswell's mother were first cousins. In fact, my good mother, God rest her soul, and Lady Haswell's mother were competing for the same beau. The Viscount Watford. But Lady Haswell's mother won out in the end." He sighed.

My father had been right. Fate had not been kind to the vicar. Though, thinking about his connection with Lady Haswell, I now wished my father had not confided in the vicar about the missing cross. What if the vicar communicated some of my parents' uncharitable suspicions, or indeed my mother's behest to me, to Lady Haswell? One could never underestimate my father's capability of revealing sensitive information to strangers.

I shifted in my seat, ill at ease, and drove on. I needed to come up with a plan about what to say if the topic of the cross came up again during the engagement party.

The road began winding its way through the Downs. Having spent so much time on the Continent of late, my heart filled with joy as I looked upon the quintessential English landscape. A patchwork of farm fields with forested fringes, meadows, and verdant valleys spread out before us. Charming villages with white houses nestled among the undulating topography. And the steeples of ancient stone churches peeked out among the hills.

Soon, we buzzed through the village of Diggles, past a pretty timbered tearoom and a quaint village pub, with a few men in suits and fedoras sitting on the outdoor tables, but didn't stop.

At the end of the village, the road forked, the main road continuing on to Canterbury. I swerved into a quiet country lane on the right and took the road to Resington Hall. Having visited once or twice, I knew my way around this part of the country. Just outside the village, the 400 acres of Resington Hall Park began. And just over the hill, I knew the landscape would open up in front of us once again, and to the left we would get our first glimpse of the house itself, situated so happily in the soft rolling hills of the Downs.

The vicar let out a small cry of surprise, and I thought he'd spied Resington Hall. But the next minute I saw two women jump, with a spring in their step, out of a kissing gate cut in the hedge on the left side of the road, and almost collide with us. My heart stumbled and for a moment I thought my aunts' prophecy had come to pass.

But the women cleared the car by mere inches, waved merrily to us, and went on their way, paying us no mind.

"Why, it's Mrs. Brown and Mrs. Green!" the vicar

exclaimed unexpectedly as I drove on.

"Who?" I asked, not recognizing the ladies myself.

"What a coincidence!" he continued, as he turned around to gaze after the women. "I met Mrs. Brown and Mrs. Green about a week ago," he said, turning forward again, "at our parish church. They are two American ladies, widows, poor things, on a brass-rubbing holiday through the British Isles. Fancy meeting them here!" He continued shaking his head, lost in contemplation of the mysterious ways of the Lord.

I threw a glance back at the women in my side-view mirror. Wearing country tweeds and binoculars, they were now climbing over a stile on the other side of the road.

Curious little questions presented themselves about the two women. But they were soon driven out by the first glimpses of Resington Hall, rising uneasily out of the gently rolling landscape.

Once the darling of Elizabethan poets who praised its beautiful white stonework and lace-like facade of tall windows, the original building had burned to the ground in 1834, and had been unfortunately replaced by a Victorian misunderstanding in the Gothic Revival style. Heavy on the red brick, turrets, and towers, it had all the charms, one imagined, of the Lowood Institution in *Jane Eyre*.

Now, instead of inspiring poets, the building

had the effect of rattling those with weaker constitutions. The vicar gave his second startled cry of the day. I smiled covertly.

I could not think of a more oppressive building in England to host an engagement party. It stood as a red gash across the bucolic Kent landscape. And what twisted Victorian mind could have imagined that such a clunky building would be a suitable summer residence? Though, to be fair, one look at the building did give one the chills, so perhaps the nameless architect had achieved his original purpose.

But even as we caught the estate's gates in our sights, something else seized my attention that chilled me even further, and I shivered despite the warm August breeze. It was not the view of the garish building that was disturbing the peaceful lane. Ahead of the car, just off to the side of the road, where the low dry stone wall marked the boundaries of Resington Hall Park, lay a dark mass.

Though crumpled and balled up like a boulder, the true essence of the shape was unmistakable— it was the body of a man.

CHAPTER 6

I stopped the car under the shade of a chestnut tree and got out to inspect the body. I looked up and down the road, but this was a deserted stretch, and was mainly used to get to the Hall. Ours was the only car. The gates of Resington Hall were just a few yards down the road, and I wondered if anyone had already gone to seek help.

At first I thought that perhaps the man had collapsed from the heat, or a heart attack, or sickness. He lay motionless, face down in the grass scrub by a stile in the wall. He wore a dark suit, akin to something a door-to-door salesman would wear. His hat had rolled away a little further down the road, probably when he had fallen to the ground.

I stepped closer and peered at him. It was obvious that he was hurt. Thoughts raced through my mind. Perhaps he had been hit by a passing automobile, but his body looked quite intact. The most likely reason for his prostrate position was the bloody gash on the back of his head.

A twig snapped nearby. I froze. *The killer!*

I leaned over the stile and scanned the footpath leading from it and down a hill towards the Hall in the dell. Skirting the path on the left was a copse of trees. And there, along its edge, coming in and out of the shadows thrown by the trees, was a dark figure, a man, hurrying away.

In his haste, he dropped something. It looked like a piece of paper—the sun shone off its white surface. As he bent down to pick it up, he looked up. Our eyes met. My heart lurched into my throat. It was James. We stood there, our eyes locked for a few moments across the distance. He then straightened up, put the note in his pocket, and trotted away.

Just then, I noticed the vicar lumbering towards me.

Encumbered by his various rolls, parcels and boxes, the vicar had taken a bit of time to disengage from the car. The roadster's low profile had also hampered his exit from the vehicle. He now puffed his way to where the body was.

I had to act fast. I did not want him to see James. Dropping my purse at my feet, I made a big show of collecting its spilled contents. No stranger to his own mishaps, the vicar good-naturedly bent down next to me to pick up my lipstick and compact mirror. I hoped that by the time we straightened up, James would have had ample time to go down the path and disappear around its bend.

Dusting off my bag and summer frock, to buy James a bit more time, I wondered what his unexpected appearance on the path leading away from the body meant.

"Oh, dear!" the vicar exclaimed, cutting into my thoughts. "Is he alright?" He was leaning over the man on the ground and seemed not to have noticed James.

"I cannot be certain," I said. For the first time, the thought crossed my mind to see whether the man was still alive. I reached out to the man's neck to check for a pulse where I thought one ought to be. Although I had seen my fair share of bodies, I had never touched a dead man. I grazed the skin of his neck, but recoiled quickly.

"But I think he is dead. We should go to the house and ask for help," I suggested, turning to look at the vicar. He was staring at the gash on the back of the man's head.

Perhaps the man was not dead, I thought, somewhat contrary to the evidence. And perhaps James had not been the one who had hit him on the head, I told myself.

The vicar fretted a bit, but agreed to stay with the body. For a man who specialized in communing with the afterlife, the vicar appeared to be quite apprehensive about being left on his own with a body. I felt strongly that we couldn't leave the man by himself on the ground, and since I was the one driving, I could get help quicker.

Plus, if the man was dead, who better to administer to his needs than the vicar? Although I didn't voice that particular thought.

The tires slipped on the gravel as I revved up the car through the gates and down the drive.

Though lost in thought about James' presence near the body, my mind was momentarily distracted by the elegant drive. Tall ancient trees stood by the side of the road like sentinel, some bowing as though to welcome guests. Driving up to the house gave the visitor the impression that one was about to come out on the other side into an enchanted land. The road meandered like a peaceful river toward the house. At the last turn, an ancient Welsh yew tree revealed itself, signaling that the house was just ahead.

Lulled into reverie by the natural beauty of the estate, the hideous Victorian monstrosity that was Resington Hall jarred one unexpectedly back to reality. The house, with its turrets, embellishments, towers, and decorative brick, was even more disagreeable up close. I once again resolved that the Victorians had a lot to answer for.

An icy shiver traveled down my spine and it took me a moment to realize that it was not the house which had elicited this response. While the clunky red brick facade itself was enough to silence anyone's heart, it was the scene I had left behind by the house's gates, which unsettled me.

The body would certainly throw the

engagement party into disarray. The official announcement of Leopold's engagement to Daphne Carter was to be tonight. I dreaded being the bearer of bad news.

I sat in the car unresolved for a moment, and wondered if I shouldn't first find James and let him explain the circumstances in which I had observed him, before speaking to his parents—Lord and Lady Haswell.

And then a new thought occurred to me. What if all of this had nothing to do with the Haswells and Resington Hall? What if James was there just by coincidence? What if the body of the person in the lane had nothing to do with this house and the people in it?

I had so quickly jumped to the conclusion that something sinister was going on that I had not stopped to consider that the presence of the man by the road might have a perfectly normal explanation. And while the man's death was an unpleasant inconvenience, it need not disrupt the planned events. The authorities would be called, and the body would be cleared away, and the engagement party would proceed as planned.

I parked the car and sat wondering vaguely why the butler had not come out to greet me and why the footmen had not come out to take my luggage. I spared the facade another glance and was rewarded with another involuntary shudder.

It was the house, I concluded, that was playing

tricks on me. It put one in mind of a Gothic novel. There was nothing sinister going on here.

I pushed away the thought about the gash on the man's head, and with a much lighter heart, I walked to the house and rang the bell.

But as I rang the bell, a movement further away, in the garden's shrubbery, caught my attention.

I trotted quickly in the direction, thinking it might be James. The retreating footsteps seemed to lead away from the house and towards the kitchen gardens and the greenhouses. As I skirted the hedge cautiously, I became aware of loud noises—shouts and banging doors—carried on the summer breeze into the peaceful gardens. They were coming from the open windows of the house.

Ignoring them for a moment, I turned my attention back to the person slipping among the bushes with uncharacteristic agility. Though I only caught a glimpse of a straw hat and what looked like a Somerset smock, I thought I recognized the figure. But before I could continue in pursuit, a loud throat-clearing behind me made me jump, and I turned around with a start.

It was the Haswells' butler. "Lady Caroline. We have been expecting you," he said with a stiff bow.

But without warning, a large shape sprang up on me from behind the butler and grabbed me by the arm. I let out a little shriek before realizing that my assailant was my chum, Poppy.

"Oh, Gassy!" she exclaimed, using one of the

several unflattering nicknames she had for me. "I'm glad you've come!" Her voice had the power of a foghorn on a clear day. What nature had endowed her with, she had further nurtured and calibrated to its natural apex through the frequent exercise of calling after wayward balls on the golf course.

I looked at Poppy with concern. A large girl of stolid constitution, it was unlike her to be so emotional so early in the day. But before I could ask for her to elaborate, she went on: "The entire house is in an absolute uproar! The most frightful thing has happened!"

CHAPTER 7

"Poppy!" I exclaimed in surprise, "What are you doing here?!"

I had not been expecting Poppy at the engagement party. She did not strike me as a close friend of either Leopold or James. Or any of the other Haswell brothers, for that matter.

"Oh, my mother and Lady Haswell were great chums at school. Much like us," she said and grabbed me with vigor by the arm and led me further into the house.

I pondered for a moment whether to rectify her erroneous notion about the root of our friendship. Poppy, whose full name was Persephone Kettering-Thrapston, had been the Head Girl at our mutual school, Boughton Monchelsea School for Girls. We had not been friends during our time at that institution, as the numerous unflattering nicknames she had bestowed upon me at the time, and continued to use most unreservedly, could attest. But we had become quite close since, so in the interest of friendship, I did not bother to correct her.

Poppy guided me deftly among servants running to and fro down the great hall, and shoved me into the relative peace of a small sitting room overlooking the garden. I sat down on a lady-sized flowery chair. In fact, the entire room struck me with its floral-themed decor and predominantly pink color.

Poppy sat prettily across from me. She was wearing some flowery Parisian confection which belied a physique rivaling that of stone put contenders at the Highland Games. Though it was a good hour or two before teatime, she offered me a spot of tea, which sat attractively arranged on a dainty table.

"I see the preparations for the engagement party are in full swing," I said, taking a sip of my tea and gesturing towards the closed doors, which managed to dull only some of the noise. Servants could be heard scuttling about, and in the distance, doors were slammed in excitement, or perhaps agitation. "I would have thought that by now everything would be settled to receive guests," I added.

"Oh, it was, it was," Poppy assured me. "I arrived yesterday afternoon, and all was well. But the most dreadful thing occurred just a short while ago, and the entire house is in an uproar!"

I lifted a quizzical eyebrow, since my mouth was full of a delightfully flaky petit four.

What sounded like dropped teacups shattering

on flagstone and tinkling of silver spoons reached my ears. Then the feet of maids running, the more measured steps of the aging butler, and the outright sprints of pageboys. This room struck me as an island of serenity—with its flowery furniture, delicate china, and the elegant carriage clock on the mantelpiece, measuring out time in graceful chimes—in a house of madness.

I vaguely wondered if the commotion in the house had anything to do with the body by the road. I was about to press Poppy about it when she cut in.

"Daphne," she began with enthusiasm, "that's the Americans' daughter," she clarified, though I was perfectly aware of the name of the bride-to-be from the invitation, "told her mother that she refuses to marry Leopold!"

"What?!" I exclaimed after hastily swallowing my second pastry.

Poppy nodded with sustained enthusiasm. "Yes! Apparently, she's had a change of heart!"

"What? Now? After she's been here, what, a week?" I asked, incredulous.

Poppy shrugged her shoulders. "Apparently."

"How do you know all of this?" I narrowed my eyes at her.

"It's been hard to miss," she said, waving a sturdy hand in the direction of the door, "what, with all the shouting and banging going on. But I also have it on good authority from Cook." She reached for a cucumber sandwich.

Poppy had the uncanny ability to ingratiate herself with the cooking staff wherever she went. I suspected it had little to do with the amiability of her character, and more with the fact that cooks everywhere took one look at her and knew she was their kind of young woman. Her heft communicated what words might fail to describe: that she was fond of good old British cooking, the kind of cooking contrived to put meat on the bone.

"Cook says, and she has it on good authority from the housekeeper, Mrs. Collins, that Daphne claims that she had been misled about Leopold." She took a dramatic pause.

"In what sense?" I asked, intrigued.

"Apparently, the engagement was brokered between Daphne's mother and Leopold's mother through an intermediary in New York, a Lady Jessop. Who, by the way, is not so keen on New York, but apparently is very keen on the distance the Atlantic affords between her and the bailiffs. Anyhow, Lady Jessop had been supplied with a photograph of Leopold for the occasion. But, as it happens, the photograph included a few other young men. James among them." Poppy leaned over closer to me, and proceeded in a whisper, though who could have overheard our conversation above the racket going on outside the door was beyond me. "Apparently, she mistook James for Leopold."

Poppy sat back with satisfaction and sunk into the decorative pillows, sipping her tea with great finesse.

My heart jumped at the mention of James' name. And a wave of dread washed over my body for a moment, but curiosity overtook me. "And Daphne only discovered her mistake now?"

"Well," Poppy began, "I'm not entirely certain what prompted Daphne to voice her mistake on the eve of the engagement party...Perhaps it was a tactical maneuver, calculated to be deployed at the most opportune moment to deliver the maximum level of destruction to the enemy." Having been brought up by a widowed father, a veteran of the Boer Wars, and having frequently accompanied him on safaris in Africa, Poppy tended to see the world as a series of war exercises.

"And thus break off the engagement at a moment when it would offer no opportunity for it to be salvaged," I completed her thought. Clever. I needed to remember that particular technique.

Poppy nodded. "Think about it. Delivering her blow on the eve of the occasion guarantees that the families would not have time to regroup and retaliate. They would have to let her break off the engagement."

I looked forward to meeting Daphne. What girl could be so scheming? What girl would wait until the last day?

"So the engagement announcement has not

gone out to the papers yet?" I asked.

"Oh, that was another source of fuss earlier in the day! Lady Haswell was about to make the telephone call to the London newspapers, to announce the engagement—"

"Why Lady Haswell? Should not the girl's mother do that?" I asked, intrigued by the break in protocol.

"Well, since they are American…" Poppy let it drop. I understood what she meant. Lady Haswell had more standing in this country and could get the engagement announcement placed in the best publications. Perhaps even *The Tatler*. "But her plans were derailed by the news that Daphne would have none of it," Poppy continued. "And it has been like this all day." She gestured towards the door.

We sat listening to the commotion beyond the doors.

"Mind you," Poppy said after a moment, "according to Cook, there have been reporters hanging about the village for the last few days. Crowding the village pub, she says. A peer of the realm is getting married, after all. The London papers were not going to wait until the actual announcement to send someone down to report on it."

I nodded. I understood the situation perfectly. It had been like that when my sister Theodora's engagement was about to be announced.

"Maybe Leopold has done something that has made Daphne realize she can't marry him," I suggested. After all, there was a leather-bound book in my London club filled with the names of eligible bachelors and their most undesirable traits. Poor Leopold had several pages devoted to him. Not that he was a bad egg. He was just a complete bore.

I did not get a response from Poppy immediately, but evidently she had been considering my remark. "You know," she said pensively, "that's quite possible...I hear that he's only interested in observing birds with his binoculars. Not shooting them. Imagine that!" Her eyebrows shot up.

I shrugged. Yes, perhaps birdwatching was not to everyone's taste and was not a desirable trait in a spouse.

"Well, I'm glad you've come, Gassy," Poppy said. "I was going quite mad, having no one to go over things with. What took you so long? I had begun to despair that you'd never come."

"Well, if my mother had her way, I wasn't going to come. But then the strangest thing occurred, and I drove down with the vicar who's on his way to Canterbury..." I stopped myself. I realized with a start that I'd become so drawn into the domestic drama of the Haswells that any thoughts of people laying face down in a ditch and James scuttling away had quickly evaporated.

"The vicar! I utterly forgot about him!" I sprang from my chair and ran to find Lady Haswell to inform her about the arrival of her cousin, the vicar, and the unfortunate body he was guarding.

CHAPTER 8

It transpired, however, that Poppy had been mistaken regarding the chances of Daphne's plan succeeding. Despite all the broken china, the engagement party went on as scheduled. I could not fathom how the mothers had managed it, but the butler arrived in the late afternoon to announce that despite rumors to the contrary, the party was to go forward as planned.

One had to admire Lady Haswell's resilience. She had not only somehow overcome Daphne's objections to Leopold, but she also received the news of the dead body by the road with stoic calmness. It appeared that if an unwilling bride could not derail an engagement, so neither could a dead body.

As the preparations for the party had been going on for months, and as guests had perhaps arrived from all over the British Isles and from as far as America, I understood Lady Haswell's reluctance to postpone the party for anything less than a *force majeure*. And an unfortunate stranger getting himself knocked on the head was not a serious enough offense to prevent Leopold's much aspired-to, and highly-improbable, engagement from going forward.

Lord Haswell's financial woes notwithstanding, the family evidently still wielded a lot of power in the neighborhood. Police questions and interviews were quickly postponed for the following day, and as no immediate connections were ascertained between the dead man and any of the guests, the police departed to look for the culprit elsewhere.

I spent the afternoon idling about the public areas of the house—the drawing room, the garden, the library—to the detriment of my party preparations, in the hopes of running into James. Though Lady Haswell had delayed the police interviews, I still needed to make up my mind about what to tell the police tomorrow. Was I going to keep James' presence near the body secret? I wanted to speak to him to find out why he'd been there.

But I was unsuccessful in tracking him down. It was as though he was hiding from me.

In the end, I went to my room to change. After all, I had to look my best for the party if I was to make any headway on the James front.

Though the police were quickly dispensed with, that did not prevent reports of the death from weaving their way through the house like a smell rising from a musty basement. Poppy barged in quite unexpectedly—dragging her lacy and beaded couture dress behind her, to the utter distress and horror of the maid who was following after her—to tell me that the dead man had been a journalist.

"One sent here to cover the event?" I asked.

She shrugged. "I actually don't know anything else," she said, letting the maid help her on with her dress. "I'm not even entirely confident how Cook knew he was a journalist. Perhaps someone had seen him at the pub."

My thoughts became a jumble of possibilities. Why would a journalist be killed the day of the engagement party? And why by the boundary of the Hall? And why was James there? What was the note he picked up? Had it been a note from the journalist?

Poppy's gasp, as the maid pulled out my dress for the evening from the closet, brought me back to the task at hand. I smiled. The dress was a corker, as they say.

"I got it on the way back from Switzerland," I told Poppy as I slipped the dress on. It was a strikingly modern chemise in pale gold lace intricately beaded in a flower pattern that skimmed my body, with a sleeveless bodice that showed off my shoulders and a skirt that just grazed my knees. "Uncle Albert and I stopped off in Paris for a day," I said.

Uncle Albert had gone to visit the *Herbier National* and its 18th century collection of

1,241 specimens brought back by Jean Baptiste Christophore Fusée Aublet from French Guiana. I had declined his generous offer to accompany him, and left the pleasure to his valet, Wilford. Instead, I arranged a visit to the equally impressive, and no less revered, collection of evening gowns at the studio of Mme Jeanne Lanvin.

And although I had not had a chance yet to speak to James since my arrival, I was confident my outfit would not fail to catch his attention this evening.

❖ ❖ ❖

Poppy and I made our way down the marble staircase. Poppy's own Parisian concoction made her look quite elegant.

Serenity had descended over the house. Gone were the shouts and bangs of earlier, replaced by politely subdued conversation and elegantly clinking cocktail glasses floating down the marble hallways as we proceeded to the Red Drawing Room, where guests had assembled before dinner.

Entering, my dress drew immediate disapproving looks from the Victorian-era guests, spinster aunts and the like, sitting along the walls. I knew the dress reminded the geriatric set of something they would wear only in the privacy of their bedroom, and then only with the lights safely extinguished. As Mme Lanvin herself had told me, only someone truly feminine could carry off the garcon look. I stood at the entrance for a few moments for full effect and I searched the room for James.

I spotted him hovering in the vicinity of his mother and avoiding my eyes. There was some schoolboy shyness about his demeanor this evening. The tan on his face and the sun-kissed waves of his dark blond hair showed that he'd spent time outdoors recently.

That thought startled me right back to seeing him walk away from the body earlier today. I shook the unpleasant thought away.

My gaze slid past James, towards his brother Leopold. Short and bespectacled, and in the process of losing his fair hair, under the lights of the chandeliers he looked almost bald. For a man about to be engaged, he did not strike me as thrilled by the prospect. Then again, one would not be thrilled to be forced to marry a girl who just hours before had refused to do so because one was not as good-looking as one's brother, and who had spent the rest of the afternoon crying because her mother would not let her break off the engagement. Or so Poppy had told me.

Looking around the room, I noticed that very few of the guests were born during the reign of Edward VII. Some perhaps even remembered William IV being king.

I was also surprised at how small the party

was. I greeted the Haswells' two middle sons and their wives across the room. But apart from the awkward group that I assumed were the Americans, everyone else seemed to be close Haswell family. Poppy and I appeared to be the only outsiders.

Perhaps Lord Haswell wanted to keep the affair private, given the nature of its transaction. Namely, that he was resorting to courting American dowry in order to keep his financial affairs afloat.

Then what are Poppy and I doing here? I wondered.

I moved further into the room and spared Lord Haswell a glance. He was standing about in an ungainly manner near his wife, attempting to engage as little as possible with the Americans. A tall, gangly fellow, Lord Haswell's long face and raised eyebrows were stuck in a perpetual expression of distaste. He was presently occupied with giving me a contemptuous look, as though he knew the real reason I was here. I wondered vaguely if he somehow knew about my father's missing cross and my mother's clandestine mission.

Lady Haswell was not too charitable in her glances towards me either. But I had to concede that she had her reasons—one for each time I had refused Leopold's offer of marriage. Presently, she disengaged from the males of her family surrounding her and approached me.

Lady Haswell gave my dress a look that my mother would have accompanied with the exclamation: "Good heavens, Caroline! What are you wearing?" Instead, she said, "Allow me to introduce Mr. and Mrs. Carter."

She led me to the group I had correctly identified as the Americans. Lady Haswell was just as haughty and bony as her husband, and her tone suggested that she found the task of introductions distasteful. Whether that was due to her dislike of me or the Americans was unclear.

I smiled at each Carter in turn. Mr. Fred Carter was a rough looking middle-aged man, with unnaturally dark hair for his age. He had the air of a former boxer about him. Though he wore a well-cut suit, it managed to look ill-fitting and cheap on him. It bulged and pulled in all the wrong places. He sat regally in an armchair, smoking a cigarette.

On the other side of the small table where Mr. Carter's ashtray rested, sat Mrs. Barbara Carter. She also displayed a set of quite pedestrian features, which were further lessened by the inexpert attempt to enhance them through indiscriminate application of jewels, starting from those in her hair pieces, and running down her neck, bosom and arms, all the way to her fingers.

Behind them stood a young, unnaturally blonde woman, who I had assumed was their daughter, Daphne, but who turned out to be a family friend. She was a young Hollywood starlet, or so I was informed, named Ruby Wilson. Next to her was Carter's son, Jack, who was actually quite dapper and a good-looking young man of about twenty, but who only seemed to have eyes for Miss Wilson. Though I found her heavily painted eyes and bright lips quite gaudy, perhaps that looked good on film, I mused.

Barely waiting for the introductions to be over, Mr. Carter addressed me in a voice booming with confidence, "So, you're the gal that found the body?" He underscored his question with an outstretched hand while still managing to hold both a whiskey tumbler and a cigarette in it.

The entire room turned to stare at me.

CHAPTER 9

I nodded in response and quickly glanced at Lady Haswell, afraid that she would disapprove of me usurping the evening. But she was currently preoccupied with holding Mr. Carter's outstretched hand in an eagle-eyed gaze, lest some whiskey or ash spilled on her carpets.

Is murder an appropriate topic for this evening? I wondered.

Scanning around the room, I sensed a general malaise. Perhaps the mood of the Haswells, and the groom-to-be in particular, had a dispiriting effect on the guests. After all, it could not be easy to be jubilant when one was told one was too ugly to marry, but then being forced to do so anyway to the very subject who had raised the initial objections.

A jaunty discussion of murder might not go amiss to liven up the mood, I conceded.

But Mr. Carter preempted me. "So, you're Evelyn's girl," he said with a chuckle, jolting my attention back to him.

Unencumbered by social graces, he was

extending a meaty, and be-ringed, hand towards me, without getting up. At least he had emptied it of the cigarette and whiskey.

I flinched at his use of my mother's Christian name, but offered him my hand in politeness. I looked to Lady Haswell in confusion, for a cue on how to proceed, but found her face an impenetrable wall, plastered with a practiced smile. It was the same smile my mother reserved for the most insufferable of guests, who nevertheless had to be humored because they were important players in my father's political career.

"Call me Fred," the man continued, "All my friends do." He let out another chuckle and sent a wink in Lord Haswell's direction, who was now perched uncomfortably on the edge of a side chair by the wall. Relegated to such a literal and metaphorical secondary position, Lord Haswell had adopted an air of complete detachment. The only indication that he was at all affected by what was transpiring was the rhythmic throbbing of a vein in his temple.

My gaze came back to rest on Mr. Carter. He was not at all what I expected from an American. My own grandfather was American, but he was as refined as any English lord. In some respects, even more so. More importantly, Mr. Carter was not at all the type of man I would have expected the Haswells to associate with. The old adage that beggars cannot be choosers was uncannily apt in their case, I mused.

The American's loud voice filled the room. He had an easy, broad smile and behaved as though he owned the place. Come to think of it, he more or less did. As my parents had hinted, and Poppy had confirmed, Mr. Carter was in the process of buying Resington Hall and Park as a gift to the newlyweds. No doubt, it was also a way to inject some cash into Lord Haswell's empty coffers.

I wondered about what kind of business Mr. Carter might be involved in. Even my mother did not know. The important point, however, at least to the Haswells, was that he had money. And lots of it.

"Just as stunning as your mother," Mr. Carter continued. Now, this was just too much! I recoiled at the inappropriate comment. I was used to straight speaking Americans and American familiarity, but this was in such bad taste.

I glanced at Mrs. Carter, who was beaming at me amiably. I cast a glance towards James, but he kept his eyes resolutely on an ugly vase on a revolting side table.

What was going on here? How much of his fortune had Lord Haswell lost exactly that everyone acted as though this oily man was the bee's knees?!

The next moment, I felt Poppy's presence by my side and some of my anxiety dissipated. *Fred* sized Poppy up, and calculating her heft, cleared his throat with a *yes, well.*

"So you found the body?" he quickly jumped back to the much more agreeable topic of murder.

I nodded, unwilling to speak to him.

"A gatecrasher, eh?" he said. "Hoping to get a piece of the action. What a nuisance. And just before the engagement."

"Hope it's not a bad omen," the actress spoke up for the first time. Though a purported actress, I noticed her inability to hide her interest in the topic of murder.

Her voice matched her look. Contrived to be child-like and endearing, rather than seductive, it was quite unbecoming. But Jack, the Carter's son, watched her with rapt attention.

Ah, that James would look at me the way Jack looked at Ruby. He followed her every move and hung on her every utterance. Each time she spoke, he glanced at her, as though he would not like to miss a word she said.

But James just avoided my glances.

"I don't know about omens, but it seems there are maniacs running around. Is that a looney bin that you have next to you?" Mr. Carter said, addressing Lord Haswell.

"It's a sanatorium," Lady Haswell corrected. "Some of the most eminent members of society are currently resting and convalescing—"

"And the police here don't carry guns," Mr.

Carter proceeded as though Lady Haswell had not spoken. "How are we supposed to feel safe? What use are gated estates, if you have lunatics running around and dying at your gates? I'll bring some of my men to guard the place and sort it out." He winked again at Lord Haswell, who looked as though the only thing on Earth he desired at the moment was for the American to stop winking at him. "Sort out that loony bin while I'm at it as well," Mr. Carter concluded.

"Well, it's no one we know, thank goodness," Lady Haswell said, steering the conversation away from Mr. Carter's plans for the Hall and Park. Perhaps she had also noticed that Lord Haswell's vein was in danger of popping. "I understand he was a journalist," she said, looking around hopefully for someone else to join the conversation, "the police inspector told me. So many of these journalists milling around now, unfortunately." She threw her husband a quick glance. Lord Haswell flinched at the mention of journalists. The press loved a good riches to rag story, especially when it involved someone with a title, and Lord Haswell had not been spared.

"I wonder what he was after?" the American said, somewhat insensitively, I thought.

"Nothing to do with us, my dear," his wife now jumped in, perhaps sensing that it was time for a different topic.

"My dear," Mrs. Carter turned to me, "we had

such fun at your mother's luncheon. I was telling my Freddy that we have to redo the house when we get back to New York. I'm not really into old things, and your mother had so many of them, but if they are good enough for your mother, they are good enough for me." She emitted a brimming laugh that sounded as though she had marbles rolling around in her throat. "That's what I'll tell my friends when they ask me why I threw out all my nice, expensive things and got so many old things."

My mother would be mortified if she knew that Mrs. Carter was about to tell the whole of New York society that she remodeled her reception rooms to match those of Lady Beasley in England.

Had all the daughters of decent American families been married off already?

But perhaps this was what passed for high society in New York. I was only familiar with the Boston society, who would only seldom admit a New Yorker in their midst. Looking at Mr. and Mrs. Carter, I was beginning to see why.

"Isn't this house just divine?!" Mrs. Carter gushed further as she looked about the room.

I noticed that every time Mrs. Carter spoke, Lady Haswell threw daggers at Lord Haswell with her eyes, as though blaming him for the predicament they found themselves in. Perhaps she had a point.

"Such class," Mrs. Carter added. "My Freddy is so generous to buy it for the kids. And so many towers!" She rolled a few more marbles in her throat.

The towers, turrets, finials, pinnacles and hood moldings were some of the features I hated most about the house. I had rarely seen a more hideous Victorian building. But I could understand how Americans would think all of these frills signified sophistication. Although impoverished, it seemed that Lord Haswell still had a nose for business. There would not be a single sane Englishman who would pay even a farthing for this estate.

"It's a swell place. So swanky. I can't wait to redecorate," Mrs. Carter added.

Just then, the lady of the moment walked in, and we were spared Mrs. Carter's description of how she would decorate the place.

All eyes turned towards Daphne. Her father stood up in haste and lumbered to her side. He took her hand delicately and placed it in the crook of his arm, ready to lead her into dinner. Whatever Mr. Carter's failings, he appeared to be a loving father.

Daphne was an elegant young woman. Tall and slim, with a sad look on her face. Her dark hair was fashionably short, and her eyes were large. A faint redness about the eyes betrayed that she had been crying.

I could tell that, like me, Daphne was no stranger to Mme Lanvin. She was wearing a black *robe de style*, a dress with a sleeveless bodice, and a full layered skirt, which was the signature silhouette of Mme Lanvin.

I spared her brother another glance. Well-dressed, elegant, well-mannered, Daphne and Jack belied their parents. Perhaps the money had not improved the parents in any discernible—or rather, positive—way, but the children had benefited from the gentrifying effects of expensive education.

Whatever Daphne's misgivings had been about marrying Leopold, they seemed to have been ironed out. She wore a serene expression and even managed to produce a shy smile when the dinner gong sounded and her father pulled her to the dining room ahead of Lord and Lady Haswell.

As we walked into dinner, I was disappointed to find that I was seated nowhere near James. If I had a more uncharitable mind, I would think that Lady Haswell was purposely keeping me separate from James.

I smiled at the vicar who took his seat next to me. I hadn't noticed the vicar before. It was only when I sat next to him that I remembered he was also present at the party. I wondered vaguely where he had been hiding in the drawing room.

Plates clanged and crystal tinkled as dinner commenced and guests began to be served. The vicar shared some sacerdotal humor with me, choking himself with glee in the process. It was going to be a long dinner.

At the salad course, the bride's father, as expected, got up and raised his glass. We all followed suit.

"To the health of my lovely Daphne, and my future son-in-law, James!"

CHAPTER 10

As the guests raised their glasses and a cacophony of well-wishes emanated from the gathered guests, I stood frozen with my glass in the air, the sudden onrush of blood pounding in my ears. As my head spun and the room darkened, I thought I was about to be sick.

I used all my willpower to regain composure. I cast an alarmed glance at James. He was staring resolutely ahead. I turned to Poppy sitting across the table with a questioning look. All she could do was shrug.

For a few moments, I thought the American had made a mistake. Surely, he got the names of Lord Haswell's sons mixed up. I stared at the faces of the Haswell family for any reaction to his error, but they all looked serene. Lady Haswell looked positively glowing.

What was the meaning of all of this? How could this have happened?

Dinner passed in a trance. I was suffocating and hot. Food felt like trying to swallow rocks. I was simply going through the motions until the moment I could respectfully leave the room. And when I saw everyone get up, I rose from the table as well.

I clutched the backs of chairs as I made my way to the ballroom, where a dance was to start. I reached out to a wall for support as I suddenly found myself unsteady on my feet. Perhaps I'd had too much to drink.

I felt someone grab me by the elbow. It was Poppy. "Now see here, Gassy," she began, "get a hold of yourself. Chin up and all that. Better luck next time. You're beating them off with a stick, usually. I'm confident you'll have no trouble finding another dashing, penniless, scarred by the horrors of war, man that you can fix. Lord knows there are many of those about. Oh, look!" she exclaimed as we reached the ballroom. "Are those Whitstable oysters? They look absolutely atrocious. Let's go try some," she said and steered me towards a table laid out with various trays.

We weaved through the crowd to the tables. It seemed that new people had crawled out of the woodwork. Or perhaps they were just guests invited to the dance. I was glad Poppy kept talking some nonsense about the food on the table because otherwise I would have broken down and cried.

Poppy deposited me by the edge of the table and I stared blankly at all the tarts and cakes on show as she sampled the fare.

"Doesn't Leopold look handsome this

evening?" she asked, jolting me out of the dark thoughts swirling in my head.

I followed the direction of her gaze. There was nothing handsome about Leopold. If anything, the lighting in the ballroom made him look even paler and balder, and lights flickered unattractively off the lenses of his glasses.

But it struck me that he did not display any hint of disappointment about what had transpired at dinner. It was as though I was the only one who heard James' name being called out. Was Leopold not aware that he was not the one getting married?

Noticing me looking at him, Leopold smiled at me. I looked hastily away.

A young man came to ask me to dance, but I declined.

"Poppy, why am I the only one surprised by this turn of events?" I said, glancing about the ballroom at all the cheerful people. James was dancing with Daphne. His back was to me, so I could not see his expression, but hers was radiant. Near them, Jack was dancing with Ruby.

"It was the talk of the kitchen all afternoon," Poppy said in a guilty undertone.

I threw her an accusatory look. And then blood rushed to my head as I comprehended her full meaning. Poppy had known this whole time and not said anything!

"Don't give me that look. I went down for a light

snack, to hold me over between tea and dinner," she said, misinterpreting my look.

"Not that," I said, groaning. "James!"

"Ah. I could not tell you, Gassy," she lamented. "You looked so lovely and pretty in your dress. It would have been a shame to let you know beforehand. You would have ruined your face."

I stared at her for a few minutes, deciding how to react. But the guilty look on her face soon assuaged some of my anger. She had acted in my best interest. There was never going to be an opportune time to let me know the James was to be engaged to someone else.

"Besides, I felt sorry for James as well," she said. "What a difficult situation to put him in. Having to choose…" she faltered.

"To choose what?" I latched onto her pause.

"You know," she said, suddenly bashful. "To choose between his duty and…"

"And his heart?" I asked, barely above a whisper. My heart was pounding. I was not certain I wanted to hear her answer. But I had to know.

"Oh, Gassy. Don't make me do this," Poppy whined.

That was all the confirmation I needed. A wave of relief and then sorrow crashed over me. Here I finally had the affirmation of what I had always suspected, or at least hoped, that James had feelings for me. But now that I had confirmation, he could never be mine. He was engaged to someone else.

Wild ideas began crashing about in my mind. Was there a way to stop the wedding?

"But I thought the American, Mr. Carter, was after a title for his daughter," I said. "Isn't he marrying off his daughter to raise his profile back in America? Surely James cannot supply Daphne with a title. The title is Leopold's birthright." Suddenly, I felt indignant on Leopold's behalf.

"Well, according to Cook," Poppy began, "his parents gave James an ultimatum. Going forward with the marriage was the only way to recoup some of the family fortune. Mr. Carter is buying this estate. Lord Haswell is depending on this money."

I was surprised about how much information Poppy had got out of the kitchen staff.

"But Lord Haswell cannot bestow a title. This estate doesn't come with a title," I countered.

"Yes, but perhaps for the Carters, being married into Lord Haswell's family is enough." Poppy shrugged. She had never been terribly interested in the intricacies of hereditary titles. "And Lord Haswell desperately needs the money. Plus," she said after taking a bite of some confection, "as her father has already agreed to buy this place, and as it was Daphne who wanted to break off the engagement, Mr. Carter had no choice but to go along with the new arrangement for a son-in-law, title or no title for his daughter. The mothers arranged it, the fathers had no objections. Still, Daphne will be The Honorable Mrs. James Haswell. Sorry, Gassy," she added after she noticed my face.

"So everything is settled then," I said and led Poppy to a chair by the wall so I could sit down. I needed to think about this. "How could James agree to such a thing?" I asked the air.

"I don't think he had much choice," Poppy answered. "It's his family duty."

"Poor Leopold," I said, my thoughts now jumping to his jilted brother.

"I thought you didn't really like him much," Poppy said.

"Not enough to marry. But I don't wish him ill. He's just a bit boring, walking around with his binoculars everywhere." I checked to see that he had not worn his binoculars with his evening attire. "He doesn't deserve to be treated like that."

"But at least he still has his title, right?" Poppy asked.

I nodded. "No one could take that from him."

We sat in silence for a few moments, blindly watching the dancing couples.

"So Leopold's wife would be called 'Lady'?" Poppy asked.

I nodded.

"He looks so lonely," Poppy said, casting him a glance.

I looked towards Leopold as well, standing by

the opposite wall, with his hands in his pockets, swaying gently to the music, as though oblivious to all that had transpired. "I have to say, he is handling the situation admirably. One would think he did not want to marry." That thought was a revelation. I stared at Leopold in a new light. Having always been the one to break off engagements, I never considered that there might be men who didn't want to marry either.

"Perhaps she was not the right girl for him," Poppy reflected. "She's too delicate and melancholy for him. What he needs is a strong woman."

And with that, Poppy got up and left me to my thoughts.

Abandoning my lonely chair by the wall as well, I walked around in a daze and went to get another drink.

A little further away, the actress, Ruby, was leaning on Mr. Carter's shoulder in quite an intimate manner. Jack was hovering nervously behind them, smoking. I frowned.

"Daphne looks so pretty tonight," Ruby was saying. "I'm so happy for her. Oh, hello Jack. What do you think?" she turned to Daphne's brother as though just noticing him, and he seemed startled by her question.

"Will you drink with me?" she asked no one in particular. "Maybe I should find myself a lord. Hollywood is only full of grabbers. Always wanting something. New love, new chance of happiness. Eh, Frank?"

"Ruby, you're drunk," Jake said, swooping to her side. "Let's get you to bed." He led her delicately out of the room.

As I watched them leave the room, two things struck me. One, that Ruby appeared far too intimate with Mr. Carter. And two, that James would never look at me again with the tenderness Jack reserved for Ruby.

CHAPTER 11

The next morning arrived as glorious as the previous, as though nothing untoward had occurred at the engagement party last night.

And with it came the police.

They materialized around breakfast time, and their presence drew my attention back to that which had so completely eluded my interest and concern ever since dinner the previous night—the dead body by the gates. As I had discovered the unfortunate man, I was interviewed first. I told them the little I'd seen. And since I still had not spoken to James, I kept his name out of my abridgment of events.

Forgoing breakfast—I had no appetite and little desire to talk to anyone—I instead decided to track down the owner of the gardening smock I had observed leaping in the bushes yesterday.

Leaving my room, I was about to walk down the stairs and out the door when soft sobs stopped me in my tracks. They were coming from the hallway on my right. As this was the corridor opposite where my own room was located, I was not certain whose rooms were to be found here.

The tactics ingrained in me while attending Frau Baumgartnerhoff's excellent finishing school were a habit difficult to cast aside. Curiosity overtook me, and I crept softly forward into the darkened hallway.

Frau Baumgartnerhoff had impressed upon her charges the importance of always keeping one's finger on the metaphorical pulse of one's household and, more importantly, on one's husband. Although, in the case of the husband, Frau Baumgartnerhoff had actually advocated keeping a foot on his neck. But that's neither here nor there. So in order to keep abreast of household matters, Frau Baumgartnerhoff taught her students how to creep about in the dark and listen at doors undetected.

I put my ear to the first door. I could hear some rustling inside, but the crying was not coming from that room. Then I went softly to the next room. I was about to put my ear to that door when a voice behind me said, "Lady Caroline?"

I jumped at the unexpected interruption. I had not heard anyone walk down the hall behind me. My training from Frau Baumgartnerhoff must be wearing off.

It was the vicar.

"Pardon my interruption of your efforts, but I had expected to see you at breakfast, and having failed to spot you, walked the hallways in search of you."

I raised a questioning eyebrow.

"I have news of great import to impart to you," the vicar said as a way of explanation.

I surveyed the vicar closely. He seemed to have grown since the last time I'd seen him. If his words were not sufficient to rouse my interest, it was the strange bulges in his vestments, and the fact that he was carrying the rolled-up tapestry under his arm, that caught my attention.

"Yes, what is it Rev. Bamford?" I asked and hoped that the blush rising up my cheek due to the embarrassment of being caught snooping was masked by the gloom of the corridor.

"Perhaps here is not the most opportune place to conduct our conversation," he said.

We descended the grand staircase and found the library deserted. We slipped inside, and the vicar closed the door with a soft click.

"I must begin by telling you that the news has prevented me from sleeping a wink last night," the vicar commenced.

I hadn't slept either. I wondered if our reasons were somehow connected. But I could not imagine the vicar being disturbed by the fact that James was getting married.

"Some valuable antiques have gone missing from this house," he said, and adjusted the bulges under his clothes. "That is why I have hidden your family's valuables upon my person, to keep them safe until our trip tomorrow to Canterbury."

"Is Lord Haswell's Order cross also missing?" I asked, confused.

"No. At least, I don't think so. Master James only mentioned some valuable silver items. But seeing how your father's cross is missing, I felt compelled to bring the incidents at Resington Hall to your attention. It was the unexpected coincidence which caught my notice."

Yes, the coincidence was uncanny, I conceded.

"What kind of things are missing?" I asked, intrigued.

"The first item Master James noticed missing was the H5 marine chronometer by John Harrison," the vicar said. Perhaps noticing the blank look on my face, he added, "It's the original instrument that enabled the calculation of longitude at sea."

"Is it valuable?" I asked in an attempt to cover my ignorance about John Harrison and his chronometer, but perhaps revealing it instead.

"Yes. Both historically and sentimentally, according to Master James. It's part of maritime history. The instrument made ship travel possible, and this specific specimen was a model hand-crafted by Harrison himself. It belonged to a Haswell ancestor."

"That's a very peculiar item to steal. Who would know its value? I certainly would not," I said with honesty. "It would have to be someone with intimate knowledge of maritime history, or at least antiques, to carry away such a specific thing, don't you think?"

"Perhaps you are right," he conceded. "It's not a piece that would catch the attention of just any thief. But then, Master James also noticed a rare and valuable silver nef missing. A perfect item to catch a thief's attention."

Although I was hazy on chronometers, I was quite familiar with nefs. We had several of these miniature gilt silver ships swimming across the dining table on stately occasions. Each was supposed to be a showpiece of a silversmith's skill and was the centerpiece of any princely collection. My mother brought them out every time she needed to impress new guests. I found them deplorable.

It appeared there was a nautical theme to these thefts at Resington Hall.

My mind jumped to the ladies we had seen in the lane yesterday, whom the vicar had recognized.

"Tell me, Rev. Bamford," I said, "the two American ladies who almost collided with our car yesterday, what do you know about them?"

"The Mrs. Brown and Mrs. Green?" he asked.

I nodded.

"Well, not much, to be sure. They are two widows on a brass-rubbing holiday. Lovely ladies. So interested in local history."

As the vicar couldn't elucidate their motives for being in the vicinity further, it was obvious that the ladies would have to remain a mystery for the time being.

But there was another peculiarity about the vicar's account that struck me. "Vicar, why has James related these incidents of missing silver to you?"

"I told him about your father's missing cross, of course," he said artlessly.

I winced. If news of the missing cross fell in the wrong hands, such as those of Lord Haswell, it could be used against my father.

"If a gang of thieves is targeting the great houses of the land," the vicar continued, "something would have to be done about it."

As much as I admired the vicar's patriotic spirit, I had to forestall his efforts. "Rev. Bamford, I hope the news of the missing cross has gone no further than James. Lord and Lady Haswell in particular should not hear about it."

"Absolutely," the vicar said, but a slight shiftiness around the eyes contradicted his categorical answer. "I understand how these little diversions play out among the aristocracy." He bowed his head slightly to show deference. But his demeanor, and the way he was avoiding my eyes, told me that Lady Haswell, at least, had already heard about the incident at our own home.

Just then, the door opened and James walked

in. He looked startled, as though not expecting to find anyone here.

"Ah, Master James," the vicar exclaimed with relief, "we were just talking about you."

I crumbled under the embarrassing implication. But could not contradict the vicar.

"I will leave you for now, Lady Caroline. Master James." He bowed to each of us in turn and fled the room, impeded somewhat in his progress by the packages under his vestments.

I'd spent the night working out ways to avoid running into James. He was the major reason why I had not gone down to breakfast. I started to leave as well.

"Caroline, please, stay," James said softly.

CHAPTER 12

I turned around and leaned against the closed door. I threw him a furtive glance.

My planned avoidance of James stemmed from the fact that I didn't know what to say to him. I didn't trust myself to say the right thing. And I didn't want him to think that I still had feelings for him because that would just complicate everything. I didn't want to jeopardize his engagement. And I didn't want to make a fool of myself, letting him see how much his engagement had unsettled me.

All of these feelings flooded as I wondered why he had asked me to remain behind. The silence between us was painful, and I cast around for ways to fill it. As I still hadn't congratulated him on his engagement, I decided that it was the civilized thing to do.

"Congratulations on your engagement," I said, trying to use my most sincere voice and a tone that did not betray my real feelings.

"Thank you," he said and lowered his eyes to avoid my gaze.

"I hope you will be very happy together," I continued with the accepted platitudes.

"Caroline…" he began, but faltered. He studied my face for a moment and I could feel myself blush.

James walked further into the library and leaned on the edge of the desk, facing me. I remained with my back pressed against the door. What was he playing at? I knew him well enough to not be worried that he would attempt any amorous advances. But what was his plan, exactly?

I narrowed my eyes at him, willing him to explain his actions.

"Caroline," he began again. I crossed my arms to show him I was not too happy with him. Well, given that he was now engaged to another girl, that was an understatement. And I was determined not to make this easy for him.

He looked around the room as if trying to collect his thoughts, and I let myself observe him without reserve. His jaw was set and his face was hardened into resolute determination. But his disheveled hair and darkened, restless eyes betrayed a brooding mind. He struck me as the personification of the tragic Byronic hero. And as I watched him wrestle with himself, I felt that there was something inevitable about how our lives were about to diverge.

"I had to do it, Caroline," he spoke softly and suddenly.

I started. My mind flashed to our meeting by the road yesterday. And the body. "Do what?" I asked. Was he confessing to murder?

"To agree to marry her," he said, and I was abruptly brought back to the cruel reality. I stood frozen, hardly daring to breathe, waiting for a confession I wasn't ready to hear. "Sometimes the needs of one's family, and the family name, come before any other considerations," he continued. He looked up at me and gazed at my face as though searching for something I could not give him. "It's my duty to my family," he concluded.

I shivered. I loathed the word 'duty' and how all manner of evil and cruel things were done in the name of duty. My brother had died doing his duty. Now James was getting married because of duty to his family.

I wanted to lash out at James. Why was he so maddeningly righteous? He didn't always have to do what's right. Why could he never do something silly, or something defiant, or something completely wrong?

Perhaps sensing my anger, he rushed on. "Although I have no feelings for her, I feel obliged to go forward with the engagement. You are probably well aware of my family's financial situation. With everything set in place, and Daphne refusing to marry Leopold, and my other two brothers married, it was the only way out my mother could think of. My father is ruined, and this is the only way for him to recuperate some of his losses and be able to show his face in the House of Lords."

Being aligned with such people as the Carters would do more to damage Lord Haswell's standing in society than a state of penury, I mused.

But what really troubled me was that James could marry someone he didn't love.

Though, perhaps for our class, love was not a prerequisite for marriage. As my mother liked to say, 'love' was a word used by those who entered into unwise unions to make themselves feel better about their ruinous choices.

"But you're not even the first-born," I objected. "How can preserving the family name and position be your responsibility?" If there was one benefit of being the youngest son of an Earl, it was being free of the demands and responsibilities of a title.

"Given Daphne's objections to Leopold, this was the compromise the two families reached. If it was acceptable to the Carters, it had to be acceptable to the Haswells. We are in no position to bargain."

"Was she really vehemently opposed to marrying Leopold?" I asked, a smile escaping me.

James nodded and smiled as well. Though it was no laughing matter, James was well aware of how young women perceived his brother. Leopold's continued betrothal failures were becoming something of London lore.

I couldn't fault Daphne. What a disappointment it must have been to make an Atlantic crossing only to find out that the athletic and handsome beau one had been eying in a photograph was actually not one's betrothed, but his brother.

My resentment towards James and the American girl melted away. Money and family obligations and expectations made things so difficult for our set. I was certain James would have been happy enough to live off the salary he earned as a private secretary with a girl he loved. But he was sacrificing his happiness for that of his family so that they could retain their position in society.

Unable to condone James' actions, but perhaps understanding his reasons behind them, I remained silent. He remained silent as well.

"Well," I cleared my throat, finding myself suddenly uneasy about being in the same room as James, and I moved to leave. As I reached for the door handle, he leaped off the desk and crossed the distance between us in a couple of bounds.

He caught my upper arm, gently. "No, Caroline, wait," he said. "There is something else I wanted to talk to you about."

"Yes?" My breath caught. I stared into his eyes, acutely aware of his proximity. I hoped he could not hear my racing heart.

"The vicar told me about your father's missing cross. Please don't get any ideas," he said, as though warning me. But I noticed a slight smirk.

Now I was confused. And perhaps a bit disappointed at the turn of topics. "What ideas?" I asked sharply.

"Oh, like taking my father's cross, for example," he said, now with a wide grin on his face.

My lips curled into a smile despite my best efforts. It was uncanny how well James knew my family! He would probably not be surprised to know that my mother suspected his father of taking our cross. Neither would he be shocked to discover that my mother had sent me here on a mission to retrieve ours, not steal theirs. But I kept those thoughts to myself.

"It's not amusing, Caroline," he continued, though he was still smiling. "I'm quite familiar with how your mother's mind works, having spent enough time at your house to have borne witness to more than one of your mother's schemes..." His voice fell away. I knew talking about my house had brought back memories of my brother Charles going on some wild goose chase at my mother's behest. It had for me as well.

James remained silent for a few moments, and I gave him time to collect himself.

But the past was a dangerous place to dwell in, and I pulled myself out of the darkening thoughts.

"James?" his mother's voice floated down the corridor.

I started, as though waking from a dream.

"You'd better go before she finds you in here with me," I said and stepped away from the door so he could exit.

"It would just about kill my father, if his cross goes missing as well," he said, now serious. "He's lost so much."

And with that, he left the room. I stayed behind for a few more minutes to gather my stray thoughts. To me, it seemed James had lost a lot more than his father had.

It was only after James had left that I realized that I'd forgotten to ask him about the body and the note he had picked up walking away from it.

CHAPTER 13

The property bordering Resington Hall was not a looney bin, as Mr. Carter yesterday had described it—somewhat astutely, given its current residents —but a convalescence home of the highest order.

And that was where I was headed now.

Not long after returning to England, Uncle Albert had eaten something deplorable and was, at the moment, sequestered, along with the rest of the members of the Royal Society for Natural History Appreciation, in this health sanatorium deep in the Kent Downs.

Ardent admirers of the work of Francis Trevelyan Buckland, the noted Victorian naturalist who had practiced the science of zoophagy—the study of fauna through eating it —the Royal Society members had inadvertently poisoned themselves with some tropical fish, of dubious freshness, imported from Japan.

Although the Royal Society counted among its members some of the most prominent peers of the British realm, and although each member had been a beacon of intellect and industry at an earlier point in life, the Society distinguished itself by making terrible collective decisions. The fish being only the latest in an unbroken chain of them, linking the Society back to its founding members in the seventeenth century.

And though I was not bullish on the prospect of finding anyone rational at the sanatorium, the walk there at least afforded an easy escape and some reprieve from the debacle of the engagement party.

Leaving the motorcar behind, I opted for a stroll through the fields under the glorious blue skies, in the hopes that the fresh air and bright sunshine might illuminate some of the mysteries that seemed to be swirling around Resington Hall.

As I ambled towards my uncle's temporary lodgings, I wondered about the connections between the body of the journalist, the missing antiques, and the mysterious American ladies. I did not allow my brain to dwell too much on what role James might have in all this.

Upon arrival at the sanatorium, and after being escorted to the garden by a frightful matron, I detected Uncle Albert in its verdant depths, sitting on a bench tucked under an oak tree. His straw hat was perched precariously on his fluffy white hair, and his gardening smock, which looked more like a nightgown, completed the slightly deranged ensemble.

"How is the convalescence proceeding?" I

asked, sitting beside him, after exchanging the necessary pleasantries.

"Oh, fine, fine," my uncle replied, ironing out an invisible crease on his gardening smock with his palm.

"Are you able to get around much?"

"Oh, you know. Here and there," he said evasively. "We're not actually meant to leave here, but I manage to slip out, and down to the village, when I can. The food here is atrocious. Porridge for breakfast and cabbage leaves for lunch and dinner. And no cakes for tea."

I doubted his account. This was one of the country's most renowned clinics, with a French chef in residence. But even if the fare leaned toward the more restrictive end of the subsistence gamut, it was no doubt more palatable than the questionable dietary choices my uncle made when unsupervised.

"How is your time at the house?" he asked in turn. "Is the engagement party a success? Several of the chaps here have a bet going that Leopold's present outing, in his bid for matrimonial merger, will be just as futile as the previous ones." He chuckled.

I was surprised to hear that Leopold's nuptial frustrations had achieved cross-generational status. "I imagine your chums will be happy then," I said. "Leopold failed to secure the deal again, as it were. It's James who got engaged."

"Oh, wonderful news! Congratulations Caroline! Why didn't you say so!? I always knew it, from the moment I saw you two together in France. He's a worthy young man."

My uncle gushed James' praises for a few more moments. Having been Uncle Albert's private secretary before I had taken over the position, my uncle had a soft spot for James.

"Not to me," I finally managed to say. "He's not engaged to me. It's to a frightful American instead."

"Oh, I'm sorry," he faltered. He looked around as though searching for a change of topic, or an escape route, but only managed to locate the tips of his slippers.

I patted his hand. "On a less somber note, I found a body by the gates yesterday," I said, and eyed him closely under the brim of my own sun hat. Having observed him on the grounds of Resington Hall, I was keen to know if he'd noticed anything strange.

"I know. Matron told us after we saw all the police cars whizzing by. Though, I didn't know it was you who'd found the body. Well done. Wait till the chaps hear that." He beamed at me. "Makes up for the tenner that body cost me."

I raised an eyebrow at him in confusion.

"Your aunts had been hinting at a death for the past few days now, sending regular telegrams to that effect. The lads and I had a bet going that it would be Lord Mantelbury." He threw a surreptitious glance in the man's direction, sitting on a nearby bench. Indeed, Lord Mantelbury looked a bit peaky. The dark under-eye shadows and virescent pallor gave the observer to understand that the placement of the bucket at his feet was not accidental. "I guess he's in the clear now," my uncle added, and shook his head in vexation.

Other members of the Royal Society seemed to have fared better and were scattered about the park. Most of them were half-buried, head first, in the rhododendron bushes framing the garden.

"What are they doing?" I asked, intrigued. Though, even before my uncle answered, I knew they were engaged in some sport related to the Society.

"Searching for the elusive *Oedemera nobilis.* Probably better known to you as the swollen-thighed beetle. Brilliant green species, bulging sacks on its hind legs," he said, gesticulating, unintentionally, somewhat lewdly. "Found only in Southern England," he concluded.

I nodded noncommittally and gave a respectful pause before steering the conversation away from coleopterans, though with my uncle the topic was never far behind. "You didn't happen to see anything suspicious yesterday at Resington Hall?"

It was his turn to eye me. "Who, me?" he said, shifting in his seat and becoming visibly flustered.

"I wasn't anywhere near that place yesterday."

"Uncle, I spotted your gardening smock among the bushes, evading me. Plus, I think you were observed not just by me," I said, thinking back to Mr. Carter's reference to loonies walking freely around the estate.

My uncle looked at his slippers, an unfaltering sign that he was hiding something. He then glanced about, but discovered, to his brief dismay, that Wilford, his valet, was not around to rescue him.

"Very well then," he said. "I was there. But you can't tell anyone."

What was my uncle playing at?

"I didn't think you are particularly interested in engagement parties per se," I said, probing.

"No, no." He waved off the suggestion. "I was there on an entirely different matter," he said, enigmatically.

For a moment, my heart leaped into my throat and I feared that my uncle was behind the disappearing antiques.

"Spying, if you must know," he added in an undertone, but his voice was laced with something akin to pride.

This was promising. Milling about Resington Park yesterday, he would have surely seen something useful. "Spying on whom?"

He looked around with a conspiratorial stealth

and leaned towards me. "On the Haswells' gardener," he whispered.

"What has the gardener to do with anything?" I exclaimed. I was used to my uncle being embroiled in some harebrained scheme or other, but spying on the staff didn't quite seem like him.

"Shh! Keep your voice down," he said. "I'm spying on him on behalf of my own gardener, Joseph. The Haswells' gardener has defeated Joseph every year for the last twelve years in the biggest marrow competition at the Royal Horticultural Society Summer Fair in Surrey. I promised him, while I'm here, to look into it. I know the Haswells' man is cheating."

Now that made more sense. My uncle could not resist the temptation of getting involved in any scheme where horticulture and punting intersected.

"Did you happen to see anyone in addition to the gardener?" I asked.

"I didn't actually see the gardener," he said evasively. "Well, I saw you, of course," he said eventually, capitulating under my stare.

"Did you see anyone else?" I pressed. "This is important. The dead body I stumbled on, it had a gash on the head that looked quite fresh."

"Surely you are not a suspect?" my uncle asked.

"No, I don't think so. I traveled down with Rev. Bamford, and he's my alibi. But the killer was probably lurking about when I got there." The thought sent a shiver down my back.

I could see my uncle herd his thoughts back to yesterday. He even took off his hat as though the effort made his head hot. The gentle summer breeze ruffled his fluffy white hair like the down of a dandelion.

"Well," he began, "when I got to the gardens, there was no one around—"

"What time was that?"

"Hard to say. I'm not altogether positive. To be honest, I'm not entirely certain what day it is…"

I knew that to be true.

"No, I tell a lie," he said, perking up. "Yesterday was the second Tuesday of August. I picked the day on purpose to go snoop in the garden. I knew the Haswells' gardener would be at the Dover Fair, displaying his marrows." He leaned back in satisfaction and seemed to have momentarily forgotten about our conversation.

"Uncle, what time did you arrive at Resington Hall?"

"Right," he said, sitting up. "I slipped away from here right after lunch. They served us boiled cabbage with nettle!"

"So, around one, would you say?" That was at least an hour before I had arrived at the house.

He nodded.

"And did you see anything or anyone?"

"When I got to the gardens, there was no one

around, as I said. But the most unpleasant racket was issuing out of the open windows of Resington Hall. Lots of shouting. And good thing too, as it gave me plenty of time to potter around in the garden shed and the vegetable patch without anyone hearing me break a few pots. And, you'd be happy to know, I found the most incriminating evidence in the greenhouse."

CHAPTER 14

I leaned in closer to Uncle Albert, poised to receive this incriminating evidence. I wondered what could have been hidden in the greenhouse. Perhaps a silver chronometer with a bloodstain?

"It was all very suspicious, you understand," Uncle Albert said, and leaned towards me so that the brims of our sun hats were now touching. "I expected the greenhouse to reek of fish and seaweed. That's how Joseph's greenhouse smells. He uses fish meal and dried seaweed to feed his marrows. But the Haswells' greenhouse was perfectly pleasant-smelling. I was highly suspicious the moment I went in." He tapped the side of his nose. "And do you know why it smelled so pleasantly?"

"Why?" I asked, although I knew we were getting further and further away from the reason I'd come to talk to my uncle.

"Because their gardener is using German-made artificial fertilizer." He made a dramatic pause. "I found the containers!"

"Is that against biggest-marrow competition

rules?" I asked, despite myself.

"Well, no. Not exactly," he conceded unwillingly. "But it's highly unpatriotic. German artificial fertilizer is made using ammonia derived from the Haber process. And the Haber process, as you know, is the same one the Germans employed during the war in order to make sufficient quantities of ammonia for their ammunition production. Ammunition used on our boys! Shame on him for using it to grow prize-winning British marrows."

My uncle was getting riled up, and perhaps rightly so, but the war was not something I wanted to discuss today.

"But what about anything related to the dead man by the gates?" I tried to corral his thoughts back to the task at hand. "Did you happen to see him meeting anyone?"

"Right," he said, adjusting his seat. "There was something...I remember that something caught my attention. I was tiptoeing by the boxwood hedge and paused to hear what the shouting was about. But could not make much out...Now, what was it that caught my attention?" He stared into the distance, trying to recall.

"Did you perhaps overhear a suspicious conversation coming through the open windows?" I asked.

"No, it could not have been that. My hearing is not very good."

"Was it someone you saw?" I prompted.

"That could not have been it, either. My vision is not as good as it used to be."

"But you saw me," I said.

My uncle stared at his slippers, glanced at me furtively, picked at a stray string on his gardening smock and sighed. "Very well, I did see someone walking about, but I couldn't see who it was," he said. "It was a man. Or at least I think it was...It could have been a woman in breeches and short hair." He shook his head. "Damn silly fashion." My uncle found the modern world often confusing.

As he would not look me in the eye, I assumed he had spotted James and was reluctant to reveal it so as not to incriminate him. I knew for a fact that Uncle Albert could spot a red helleborine—a rare orchid found in only three locations in the south—from a hundred paces. I doubted he could not tell whether he saw a man or a woman.

"Was this person walking toward the gates, where the body was?" I prompted.

My uncle didn't reply immediately, and I got the impression that he was deciding on what to reveal and what to keep to himself. "I can't be positive," he said and shook his head. "I was preoccupied with other matters...But there was a lot of activity near the woods," he added as a peace offering.

"The woods?" That was an interesting development.

"Well, yes. Let's see. It was just as I was coming down the hill from this place that I saw Leopold go into the woods. He looked like he was going birdwatching. A big pair of binoculars hung around his neck. Rumor has it that there is a pair of nesting short-toed snake eagles in the woods. I haven't confirmed the sighting yet myself, what with the marrow operation...But it seems young Leopold is on bird alert. Good thing the engagement fell through. Now he can devote his full attention to the birds..."

I nodded. The mention of the woods made me think back to the two women that had almost collided with the car. "You didn't happen to see two older women in the vicinity of the woods yesterday? In tweeds and binoculars?"

"Oh, the Mrs. Brown and Mrs. Green?" my uncle asked.

"You know them?!" I asked, incredulous.

"Yes, met them in the village," he said cheerfully. "Quite friendly. Seemed very interested to know more when I told them we have an American in our family. Your mother," he added, in case I had any doubt who he was referring to. "Though it's nothing to boast about, I thought the information would please them...On a brass rubbing holiday. Very interested in history. Seemed particularly fascinated by your father's missing cross."

"What?!" I asked. "How do you know

about that?" I couldn't believe that even those sequestered deep in the Kentish countryside knew about my father's missing cross.

"Your mother telephoned to enquire if any of the Lords at the clinic were at death's door, or at least incapacitated enough not to be able to attend the Order's meeting, and whether any of them would mind lending a cross to your father. Just for the meeting, you see, until a replica can be made."

Was there a living soul in Kent who didn't know about the missing cross? How was one to go about undetected when everyone knew about it?

"But why would you tell two strange women about it?" I asked, outraged at his imprudence.

"Was it a secret?" my uncle asked, his eyes widening.

I shook my head. There was no point arguing over it. "I wonder what they were doing in the woods yesterday?" I said instead.

"Not birdwatching, I can tell you," my uncle said. I looked at him sharply. "I don't know much about brass church plaques, but I know those two women know nothing about birds," he scoffed.

Uncle Albert launched into a complicated explanation about feather patterns on British warblers or bee-eaters or the like. And while I could not follow the specific and convoluted exposition, I had no doubt that my uncle was correct in his assessment of the women.

"There is something suspicious about those

two ladies," he concluded. "If you ask me, those binoculars are a cover."

"For what?"

My uncle just shrugged his feeble shoulders.

I wondered why, if he was suspicious of the two women, he had told them about my father's cross. But as we sat in companionable silence, and I watched the breeze tousle his white hair, I knew that his thoughts would by now be scattered on the wind like the seeds of a dandelion.

I got up to take my leave.

"You know, Caroline," Uncle Albert said, "I don't understand why young women are so opposed to Leopold. No man who is a birdwatcher can be inherently bad. Your aunts would have fared far better if they had married birdwatchers."

Perhaps there was some truth in that.

Something about my uncle's comment crystalized an idea that had been rattling around in my brain. "May I borrow your binoculars?" I asked.

"Ah, thinking of taking up birdwatching? Wise choice," he said and surrendered the equipment hidden deep in the folds of his gown. "No quicker way to a man's heart than through birdwatching."

"Something like that," I answered, and leaned in to kiss him on the cheek in lieu of goodbye.

Reluctant to face the fierce matron again, I opted for climbing over the low hedge. But just as

I had one leg over the shrubs, in a most unladylike manner, my uncle's voice halted my pursuit.

"I got it!" he exclaimed.

"What did you get?" I called back, thinking he'd captured a swollen-horn beetle.

"The strange thing I noticed," he bellowed. "It came back to me!"

I trotted swiftly to his side.

"It was a smell!" he said, excitement coloring his voice.

"A smell?" I asked, perplexed.

"Yes. Nasty smell. Cigarettes!"

I looked at him disapprovingly. "Cigarette smell? Why is that strange?"

"No gentleman would smoke a cigarette, Caroline," my uncle replied, his voice slightly acerbic, as though hurt by my skepticism. "Gentlemen smoke cigars. After dinner. With whiskey."

My uncle was a man of a different century, so there was little use pointing out that cigarette smoking was quite *de rigueur* nowadays. Most young people from our set smoked.

"I don't know what riff-raff they have staying at that house. Smoking cigarettes in the garden during the day, like a common laborer." He shook his head.

Perhaps there were subtleties about smoking etiquette that were not obvious to me, but were significant to my uncle. Not for the first time did I wonder about how different the modern world must seem to Uncle Albert.

I smiled at him. "So someone was smoking a cigarette in the garden in the hour or so before the man was killed by the gate?"

He nodded.

"Thank you for the clue," I said, and leaned it to kiss him on the cheek one more time.

As I bustled over the hedge, I mused that only my uncle would think that there was something disreputable and suspicious about cigarette smoke.

CHAPTER 15

Putting the cigarette smoke to one side, there were a few interesting tidbits that had materialized out of the conversation with my uncle, namely the presence of the American ladies in the woods. If my uncle was correct, and they were not there to observe a nesting bird, what was their role in this mystery concerning a dead journalist and missing antiques?

Most likely the two women were the thieves responsible for the disappearing valuables at Resington Hall. That would also explain their interest in my father's cross. Whether they had a hand in the murder of the journalist remained to be seen.

I wondered if the journalist had gotten wind of the missing antiques and was killed to prevent him from going with the information to the police.

As I ambled back to the house, I tried to see the land as my uncle would have seen it yesterday. The Haswells' estate spread laconically across the landscape as I paused at the top of a hill. I could read it like a map.

From my high vantage point, a vast expanse of hills and fields, a medley of varying shades of sun-drenched greens and golds, stretched to the horizon. Sheep dotted the fields like clouds. Birds swooped from the sky and danced on the soft breeze.

The village of Diggles, just a cluster of stone houses, stood to the right, hidden mostly from view by the woods. To the left was Resington Hall. Just ahead were the gardens, starting with the formal gardens next to the house, enclosed by boxwood, continuing with the less formal gardens, then the vegetable patch and kitchen gardens, ending with the greenhouse. And past the gardens, lay the woods.

Coming from the sanatorium, Uncle Albert would have seen Leopold going into the woods, then the two American women after him. Were they following Leopold, or were they using the woods to observe someone else in the house? If they had not bumped off the journalist, had they witnessed who had?

From here, one could also make out the meandering drive from the gates to the house, though most of it was hidden from view by the trees lining its sides. The walking path where I'd seen James, by the edge of the woods, was also visible.

Though shrubs and trees obscured most of the low stone wall at the boundary of the estate, I could see clearly the area where I had found the body. Policemen, no bigger than black ants, were searching the thicket and undergrowth lining the road for clues.

I had to concede that it would be difficult to see with any certainty exactly who was walking to and back from the place where I had found the body.

I rambled down the hill towards the house, crossing a cheerful stream over a footbridge. Walking through meadows filled with wildflowers, and then the gently sloping lawns of the English garden, brought me to the tall boxwood hedge bordering the formal gardens.

This was probably the path my uncle had taken. I paused by the hedge and surveyed the land again. The walled kitchen gardens and the greenhouses were to my right. That would have been my uncle's ultimate destination yesterday. But he would have paused right about here, and he would have spied James walking along the path by the woods.

As I lingered, trying to reconstruct my uncle's view, I heard agitated voices drifting on the breeze. Someone was speaking near an open window. I moved closer to the hedge to hear.

One would normally not eavesdrop on other guests at a country house, but since there had been a murder, I quickly decided that the rules of decorum did not apply.

As I strained to hear, I tried to recollect which part of the house would be facing this way. If my calculations were correct, this was the side where most of the guest bedrooms were located. Just below was the morning room. And although I could not see over the hedge, I could surmise that the voices were coming from the bedrooms above, rather than the morning room.

"I'm sick of covering for you. I'm always being made out as the bad guy," a young woman with an American accent was saying. It took me a moment to realize that it was the actress, Ruby. "They know about my meeting with him. One of his journalist buddies recognized me from the village tavern. And now they found the brooch in his room as well. You have to come clean. Do you hear me?"

She was talking about the dead journalist!

"I can't," came the voice of Daphne. It was feeble and full of fear.

"Or I will," the actress threatened, but not with real malice.

"Oh, please, no," Daphne cried desperately. "It will be the end of me."

"You've got to tell them about the brooch, at least. Okay?" the actress said.

The repeated mention of the brooch caught my attention. Was that yet another thing that had gone missing from the house? Had the journalist been a thief? But why was Daphne so frightened of telling the police about it? And why had Ruby met the dead man at the village pub?

"He would not have stopped at the brooch, you

know that," answered Daphne.

"None of that matters now. He's dead," said Ruby sternly, as though a tutor reprimanding a child. "I'll tell them I was meeting with him at the tavern because he was pestering me about a Hollywood story. But you've gotta tell them how he got the brooch. Promise me. Because right now it's looking bad for me."

"Okay. I will," said Daphne.

"You don't have to tell them everything. Just enough to explain why he had my brooch on him," said the actress.

"Are you done with that?" Daphne asked. "Close the window before someone overhears us."

Just then, I caught the smell of cigarettes. Ruby had been smoking at the open window. *Of course, that's what my uncle had smelled.* Someone had been smoking from their bedroom window yesterday when my uncle was snooping. It could have been Ruby. But it also could have been Mr. Carter. He had alluded to seeing my uncle around.

The window closed. It was clear I would not get to hear the rest of their plan. I moved away quietly in the direction of the greenhouse.

As I walked away, I thought I heard another window close as well.

"Where have you been all morning?" a voice hit me like a bullet in the back of the head. It was Poppy.

"Oh, hello, Poppy. I went to visit Uncle Albert,"

I said defensively. "I didn't think you'd want to join me."

"Perhaps not. But I would've liked to have been asked, all the same," she huffed.

"By the way, I brought you these," I said and handed her Uncle Albert's binoculars, hoping that would appease her.

"What am I supposed to do with them?" she asked, eying the binoculars suspiciously.

I shrugged. "Perhaps you want to take up birdwatching while you're here?" I suggested.

Poppy huffed again, but took the binoculars nevertheless. We walked amiably back to the house, Poppy fiddling with the knobs of the binoculars, and I lost in my thoughts.

The conversation I'd overheard played over and over in my mind, and I wondered what it all meant.

Questions swirled in my head. Why had Ruby given the journalist her brooch? Or had he stolen it?

And what was so special about the brooch? Did it have some special meaning? Did it incriminate Ruby, or Daphne, in some way?

Why had the actress met the journalist at the pub? Surely she knew someone would recognize her. Was he working on a story? Was it about Ruby? But then why did she say she was covering for Daphne? Was the story about Daphne?

Clearly, on the day of his murder, the journalist

had been loitering by the gates in the hopes of meeting someone. Was it a pre-arranged meeting, or was he hoping to run into someone on the off chance?

Had my uncle smelled Ruby's cigarettes yesterday? Had she been calming her nerves with a cigarette before a meeting with the journalist? If she'd killed him, had she planned to attack him or had it been self defense?

He would not have stopped at the brooch, Daphne had said. The more I thought about it, the more it sounded as though the dead journalist had been blackmailing the actress. What was her secret? And more importantly, had she killed the journalist to keep her secret?

My thoughts drifted back to the way she had acted around Mr. Carter the previous night. Was there some sort of dark and sordid love story that the journalist had uncovered?

But then, what was Daphne's role in all of this? What did Ruby want Daphne to tell the police? What did she want her to explain to the police about the brooch? And why was Daphne so loath to do it?

And there seemed to be more to the secret between Ruby and Daphne. It wasn't just about the brooch. The actress had clearly said 'the rest' did not matter now that the journalist was dead. What exactly was 'the rest' Ruby had referred to?

I walked lost in thought, following Poppy,

half listening to her recount of the morning's events. Although I didn't have any answers to my questions, I knew that Ruby and Daphne were clearly hiding something from the police.

CHAPTER 16

The afternoon passed in a blur. Poppy brought me up to date on the latest developments at the house.

Indeed, matters were not looking good for the actress. As I'd overheard in the garden, the police had discovered Ruby's brooch in the dead man's room at the village inn, and they had learned about her meeting with him at the pub.

The only new piece of information I acquired from Poppy was that the dead man's name was Lance Bradford.

I wondered why, with so much incriminating evidence against her scattered around the immediate locale, Ruby would then proceed to murder the journalist. Surely she knew that the police would learn about her meeting with this Lance Bradford and the brooch. If she were the killer, what had driven her to such desperation?

For no more than a few moments, I also mused whether James could be involved in this whole sordid affair. But I quickly disposed of such traitorous thoughts and decided that he had simply been at the wrong place at the wrong time.

Though the note he had picked up still troubled me.

I spared a thought for the mysterious American women loitering in the woods as well. But as no one at Resington Hall, besides the vicar and myself, seemed to be aware of their existence, and as I could not fit them comfortably in my theory —were they blackmailers as well?—I quickly dismissed them.

As the day progressed, however, I resolved that the incident by the country lane, though gripping, seemed to be a matter between Lance Bradford and the actress, and as the police appeared to be doing a remarkable job identifying clues and motives, it was of no concern to me.

A somber mood weighed heavily over dinner. The atmosphere was enlivened only by frequent accusatory glances darting across the table. While I avoided looking at James and Daphne, who was sitting by his side, I harbored a morbid curiosity regarding Ruby, and noticed her slinging murderous looks at Daphne, who in turn evaded her stares. And though the exchange of glances was riveting, little was said. Everyone ate in silence, and the murder of the journalist was not discussed.

The only thing that made dinner bearable was the thought that someone other than James was likely responsible for the death of the journalist.

Ruby had proceeded to drink too much again, and talked about true friendship, which made everyone visibly uncomfortable, and she was soon dispatched to bed.

Having observed Ruby during dinner, I was convinced that there was a secret hidden among the Americans. My heart went out to Ruby—what foolish thing had she done to get herself in this mess? But I also hoped that the journalist's killer would soon be arrested, and we could all go home.

I longed to leave Resington Hall behind, and abandon James and the Haswells to their fate. Though, truth be told, I could not quiet the suspicion that James had somehow gotten himself mixed up in something unseemly.

But alas, I could not go home quite yet. Although the police might let me leave, I was still obliged to bring the vicar to Canterbury. And though I had volunteered wholeheartedly for the mission, I had begun to resent it and the whole engagement party.

Another bright and cheery morning sprang upon us, quite contrary to my mood.

The vicar—whose own mood was as jolly as a bird with a worm—pottered around with his boxes, rugs, ampules and amulets, trying to find a place for them in the two-seater. I had invited

Poppy along, but she elected to forgo the pleasure of the vicar's company and instead headed to the woods with her new binoculars. I hoped she might inadvertently resolve the mystery of the two American women, but did not charge her with the task.

We soon departed, and the closer we got to Canterbury, the more exultant the vicar grew. He was effervescing about seeing some English saint or other, being assembled whole once again for the first time since bits and pieces of him—a finger here, a vocal cord there—had been dispatched to the great cathedrals of the British Isles, five hundred years ago.

But I had to admit that even for me, Canterbury held some excitement. It was the current home of Louisa, a chum I'd met during my stint at the London typing school. My mother had secured a respectable position for her, in the manner of all the other friends I'd met at the typing course, in an attempt to lessen the shame of having a typist for a daughter.

Louisa now worked as a secretary in the office of the Dean of Canterbury Cathedral. She had been instrumental in helping me figure out some recent murderous puzzles, and I could not wait to see her again.

Cresting over a hill, we caught our first view of the cathedral, which elicited greater joy in the vicar than in me. Passing over the River Stour and under Westgate—the last remaining of the city's gates—with its round towers and a massive portal, we made our way up High Street. Ancient dwellings greeted us on either side, offering lodgings, eateries, and trinket shops for pilgrims since times medieval.

I parked the car just outside Christ Church Gateway. We were to make our way by foot into the walled Precincts, and to the Deanery, where the colloquium of vicarial riches was to take place.

"Hello," two cheery voices rang out in the narrow road.

I turned around to see the two women I'd almost run over waving enthusiastically at us from the other side of the street. As the vicar waved back, they loped across the road to join us.

"Mrs. Brown and Mrs. Green! What a delight to see you again," the vicar cried out.

As the vicar introduced us, I tried to unknot the crease of skepticism that had taken residence on my brow. My uncle's warning that the women were not what they seemed came back to me. I spared them a closer look.

Standing in front of me were two quite unremarkable middle-aged women: country tweeds, practical haircuts under their hats, sensible walking shoes, and no trace of makeup or adornments. But there was indeed something about them that reminded one of confidence tricksters. Their easy smiles and cheery disposition belied a steely gaze. Their eyes missed none of the vicar's brown packages.

As they offered to help carry the vicar's wares to the Deanery, my unease about them only increased. Why were these ladies popping up everywhere? Had they followed us here? But to what end?

Vague thoughts of missing antiques and dead journalists began to swirl in my head. Even the fact that there was a meeting here today of vicars from across the land, in possession of the most exquisite reliquary, seemed somehow significant.

The two women, however, left us without much fuss by the Deanery's door, and as I tallied the vicar's packages, it appeared as though they had not pilfered any.

But if I had been disconcerted by meeting the two American women, it was what I saw at the Deanery that completely discombobulated me.

Greeting each vicar, and relieving each of his treasures in turn, was none other than an old acquaintance—Rev. Horatio Quinton.

He acknowledged me most politely, and a casual observer would not have suspected that our paths had crossed in Italy under quite regrettable circumstances. Given what had occurred there, I was sincerely surprised to find him here, in charge, it seemed, of so many priceless body parts.

Anxious thoughts pestered me as I eyed Rev. Quinton. I followed his hands with distrust while he unpacked the vicar's merchandise and laid it out on a long oak table, which resembled a macabre banquet, crowded with gilded bones, and golden cups and plates.

While the vicar was eulogizing to Rev. Quinton about his contributions to the bazaar, I spied Louisa across the room. She had lost none of her radiance since I'd last seen her. Petite with sparkling green eyes, her dark curls were arranged artistically into a short bob. Her bright floral frock stood in stark contrast to the sea of black vestments surrounding her.

After a brief greeting, I pulled her aside.

"What is Rev. Quinton doing here?" I asked. I briefed her on my suspicions—the dead journalist, the missing antiques, the two American ladies, and now, to top it all off, Rev. Horatio Quinton. No respectable parish should deign to employ him, so I wondered at the wisdom of having him at a symposium where so many shiny pieces could tempt him.

"The archbishop has taken quite a liking to him," Louisa said.

"It's the hair, isn't it?" I asked. Rev. Quinton possessed a lion's mane quite unlike any clergy I'd seen.

In the interest of accuracy, the Rev. Quinton's good looks extended beyond the hair. Not only was his attractiveness uncustomary for a clergyman, but his visage would be the envy of most

Hollywood actors. All the men of the cloth who milled about the room paled in comparison, but none stacked up against him as poorly as our own vicar.

"No need to worry, Caroline," Louisa said. "I've been keeping an eye on him. But he seems to have renounced his ways since Italy. Perhaps it's his wife. They say his dog collar is attached to a rather short leash."

I could believe that. Mrs. Rev. Horatio Quinton, Olive to her friends—though I doubted she had any—was a force to be reckoned with. She had quite high expectations of her husband, and would let no one stand in the way of her ambitions, especially not her husband and his shortcomings of character.

On reflection, given Rev. Quinton's past, and the special skills and knowledge he had proven to possess, he was indeed an excellent judge of which bits and bobs present here today were the most valuable, and could advise the Archbishop accordingly.

As it promised to be a long and tedious day, and after arranging for a date with Louisa, and after her assurance that she would keep an eye on my family's treasures, I slipped out of the walled Precincts and into the lively streets, frothing with modern-day pilgrims, of Canterbury. Perhaps I would even catch another glimpse of the suspicious American women.

CHAPTER 17

"Lady Caroline," a male voice called behind me as I weighed the merits of several tearooms in front of me.

I turned around to see a man in a crumpled brown suit, which unmistakably signaled a policeman. But since most of those were up at Resington Hall, I revised my estimation and settled on a journalist.

A pair of sharp, dark, somewhat familiar eyes peered from under a worn fedora.

"Yes?" I said, uncertain how this man knew me.

"Arthur, Arthur Lancaster. From *The Tatler*," he said, tipping his hat.

Of course, now I remembered him! He had come to our house to do a piece on me, on occasion of my coming out party. Nice man. Though the raw and punchy prose he had used gave one the distinct feeling that he would have preferred to report from the battlefields of Afghanistan during the Third Afghan War. Or Belfast, at least.

Seen in the harsh light of reason, however, societal reports were no less fraught with danger.

Perhaps that's what had attracted him to the job.

One only had to recall the events of Seraphina Roehampton's coming-out ball, to appreciate the precarious situation that magazine reporters found themselves in at such events. No fewer than three reporters, who stood in the way of debutants who had been starving themselves for months to fit into the latest Parisian couture gowns, were trampled over when the canapes were brought out.

My own coming out party had been perhaps less perilous, though no less eventful. But that's a story for another day. Suffice to say that I was not surprised in the least that Mr. Lancaster remembered me.

"Mr. Lancaster. Of course! Nice to see you again," I said. The intervening years had weathered him, but he retained his thick brown mustache and his kindly, avuncular demeanor. "How is the leg?" I enquired politely.

"Oh, much better. Thank you for asking," he said. "It's only a limp now. The wife says it's barely noticeable."

I beamed my best smile at him and urged him to give my best to his wife. Following my debut ball, my mother had thought it prudent to invite Mr. and Mrs. Lancaster to afternoon tea, to smooth things over and remain in the good graces of the press, in the hopes that with time, the leg would heal. I was glad to hear it had.

"Pardon the presumption, Lady Caroline," he

said, cutting into my thoughts, "but are you perhaps here for the engagement of Miss Daphne Carter and the Hon. James Haswell?"

Under normal circumstances I would not have presumed to divulge such information, but as my mother still felt obliged to send the Lancasters a card every Christmas, and a basket from Fortnum and Mason on Mr. Lancaster's birthday, I felt that answering a few questions and posing for a few photographs was the least I could do for him.

I nodded and smiled.

"Perhaps you would care to join me for a cup of tea?" he said.

Suspicious of journalists in general, my reservations did not extend to Mr. Lancaster. We had developed quite the rapport while I had been visiting him in hospital for the two months after my party. I was confident that he would use his discretion with whatever information I supplied to him.

I agreed to join him for tea and he led the way to a teashop nearby. We chose a table in a secluded corner and dove in.

Luckily, as a seasoned reporter, Mr. Lancaster was just as interested in talking about dinner menus and dress designers as about bodies by gates. And after we exchanged notes on guests and I relayed a few harmless anecdotes, I had no difficulty steering the conversation towards the murder.

"It's a shame about the dead body," I said. "What a way to spoil a party." I was keenly aware that the dead man had been a journalist and wondered if Mr. Lancaster could shed some light on possible reasons for his murder. So far, I'd only had the opportunity to ponder the dead man's likely connections to the guests. But what if the reason for his death was to be found beyond the walls of Resington Hall?

"They say he was found by one of the guests," Mr. Lancaster said, probing uncomfortably close to the truth.

"Oh, no. I'm positive that's quite wrong," I said, dismissing the idea. My name had been kept out of the papers on all previous occasions when I had found myself entangled in murder mysteries, and as much as I liked Mr. Lancaster, I did not intend to make him my confidante. "I'm quite certain it was a servant."

Finding him momentarily unsettled by the thought that he was in possession of inaccurate information, I saw my chance to probe Mr. Lancaster in turn. "I heard he was a colleague of yours," I said.

He visibly bristled at the suggestion. "He was no colleague of mine," he said, a dark cloud of distress passing over his face.

"I didn't mean to cause offense," I said, surprised by his strong reaction. I had not meant anything beyond the fact that the dead man had also been a journalist.

When I explained as much, Mr. Lancaster apologized and offered an explanation of his own. "He was a scoundrel. Brought shame to the profession. I'm not surprised he's dead!"

The new revelation about the dead man's character was unexpected. But I did not interrupt Mr. Lancaster, and simply raised a quizzical eyebrow at his statement.

It was only now, when Mr. Lancaster was agitated, that I noticed his traveling right eye. My mother had said that unlike the bone break, the crossed eye with which Mr. Lancaster had found himself burdened after my party would be more difficult to correct. And in the end, the problem had required visits to the surgery of a pioneering ophthalmologist, and thus an extended stay, in Vienna to correct it.

Mrs. Lancaster had been quite taken with Vienna, and my mother felt compelled to include an invitation to the Viennese Ball each year inside the Lancasters' annual Christmas card.

I tried not to stare. The doctor had done a remarkable job.

"I'm sorry for my outburst, Lady Caroline," Mr. Lancaster said, regaining his composure. "What I had meant to say is that he was not well respected by other journalists. He called himself a journalist, but he was really more adept at ferreting secrets than writing articles. He was employed by the less scrupulous publishers to dig out scandals."

"Really?" I said, and leaned in closer to hear more.

He nodded. "I tell you, Lady Caroline, there were rumors that he used nefarious methods to get his scoop."

"How do you mean?" I asked, intrigued.

"Breaking and entering. He would even keep back from his employers some of the stories he'd uncover and use them to blackmail the parties involved."

"I had no idea!" I exclaimed.

Mr. Lancaster nodded, as though to assure me that all of his information was quite accurate.

More and more ideas were forming in my mind. The dead journalist was turning out to be quite an interesting victim.

"But what was his background?" I asked. "Where did he pick up all of these criminal tendencies?"

"He was a bit cagey about his past. Though he had a funny trick—he could switch between British and American English with ease. A bit like your mother."

I nodded and smiled.

"They say he spent some time in America," Mr. Lancaster continued. "Ran around with thugs. Apparently, he was afraid of going back to America. Lord only knows what he'd done.

Probably killed someone. Or at least that's what they say."

Just then, the bell of the teashop chimed rather forcefully.

A journalist breezed in and scanned the establishment, as though looking for someone. All eyes turned to him. He latched onto my companion and walked up to our table briskly.

"Arthur!" he exclaimed. "Where have you been hiding? What are you doing in a tearoom?" The newly arrived journalist threw me a dubious glance. "I need your car," he turned his attention back to Mr. Lancaster. "There has been a development at the great house. We have to go," the man urged.

CHAPTER 18

Mr. Lancaster hesitated for a moment. He glanced back at me, as though deciding what to do. I could understand his dilemma. On the one hand, there was some development at the house, on the other, I was a guest at that house who might be able to throw some light on the new development.

"Do you need a lift, Lady Caroline?" he asked. I declined.

In the end, he left with his colleague.

It seemed that most of the patrons had the same idea, as they all got up and left in the wake of the journalists. I wasn't certain whether all of them were journalists, but it was clear that all of them were interested in learning about what had happened at the house.

The few more astute among them threw me a furtive look. They probably knew I was a guest at Resington Hall and wondered if I was in possession of some privileged knowledge about the events that had transpired. But the truth was that I was as much in the dark about what had gotten the journalists so excited as any of them.

Unhappily, I had to wait until the vicar's colloquium ended for the day to drive him back.

I did not waste my time idly, however. I sat and wondered about what might have happened at the house. I wondered if the police had finally made an arrest for the murder of the journalist. But if they had, that meant that the killer was someone at the house. Was it the actress? Or James? I swatted that thought away like a pesky fly.

But the thought that the Haswells might be involved in this sordid affair would not leave me. If the journalist was a blackmailer, was he blackmailing one of the Haswells? Would that explain the missing antiques?

Displeased with the implications of these thoughts, I turned my musings instead to more agreeable matters. If Mr. Lancaster's information was correct, and I had no reason to doubt him, the strange events at Resington Hall seemed to be connected with America.

This new information was a confirmation of what I'd already suspected, that the dead journalist was privy to some ruinous information about Ruby and had been blackmailing her. *Or had he been blackmailing Daphne?* I wondered, thinking back to the conversation I'd overheard. There had been fear in Daphne's voice about some truth coming to light. What did the two young women so desperately want to keep secret?

And had the dead journalist really killed someone in America? If he had, why had he been free? Surely the British police would have arrested him and transported him back to America.

What if the journalist had discovered something about the Carters during his time in America? What if he was killed because he knew something about the family that they wanted to keep secret? Politicians, which was what Mr. Carter was trying to be, were notorious for hiding secrets.

And now that I knew that the journalist had a connection to America, the persistent presence of the two older American ladies also grew in significance. What was their connection to the dead journalist?

I spent a few happy hours going over possibilities, speculating over connections and motives, which grew more outrageous and unlikely as time passed. By the time I met up with the vicar, I was working on a theory involving an Arabian sheikh.

But as the vicar joined me in a state of exhilaration following his colloquium, it didn't seem decorous to interrupt his rhapsody about the very great pleasure which a pair of fine finger bones could bestow on a country vicar. So it wasn't until we had driven back, crossed the gates—with the police parting the crowd of journalists and onlookers—that we were able to discover what had happened at Resington Hall.

"Gassy!" Poppy exclaimed. She must have been waiting by the portico because she ran towards me the moment I'd parked the roadster. "Vicar," she said, greeting him as he alighted from the car.

"Excuse me," he said, and bowed slightly. "I fear I'm needed inside." He hurried into the depths of the house, having sensed that something requiring his spiritual counsel had transpired during our absence.

As I had no need for the vicar's counsel, I let myself be guided by Poppy into the gardens instead.

"I thought you'd be back sooner," she criticized, like a petulant child. "I'd had no one to discuss matters with."

"We drove back as fast as we could after hearing the news."

"Oh," she said, her voice deflated. "So you've heard?"

"Only that something dramatic has happened at the house. But I don't know the details. The local journalists seem all aflutter, though." I gestured towards the gates.

Her despondent expression lifted. "Well, you missed a terribly good show, Gassy! For once, I was the one who found the body!"

"A body?!" I asked, shocked. I had been expecting an arrest. I had not even imagined that it could be a second body.

"Oh, didn't I say?" Poppy said, feigning

innocence. But I could tell she was enjoying herself. In a macabre sort of way, of course. "It's the actress! I found her in the pool this morning, after pottering around in the forest with the binoculars a bit. I actually first spied her with the binoculars! Jolly useful, these!"

"Oh, Poppy! How are you holding up?"

"Never better, old girl? Why?" Poppy asked in bewilderment.

"It must have been ghastly," I said sympathetically. "It was no picnic finding the dead journalist. I could just imagine that finding a body in the water would be even more disconcerting. Although I've seen my fair share of bodies, I've always imagined that finding a drowned person would be most unsettling." I shuddered.

"Nothing like that, old stick! It brought back a bit of the safari spirit, the thrill of adventure!" she said and puffed out her chest.

"But it means the killer is most likely someone in the house," I said, maneuvering the conversation back to the topic at hand.

"Well, according to the doctor, there is no indication that she did not just fall in. She was quite pickled last night. But just as a precaution, I reconnoitered the house while waiting for you to show up, and have located an item in each room that could serve as a deadly weapon in a pinch."

Poppy rattled off a list of the items she had discovered as we walked past some topiaries.

"Swords and lances on the western wall of the great hall. A crossbow on the eastern wall of the oak drawing room. A couple of daggers in the library. I even managed to locate a score of caltrops —metal spikes one does not want stuck to one's foot, trust me, Gassy," she clarified, in response to my befuddled look. "According to the butler, the current crop of caltrops came with the dowry of a niece of Philip, the Duke of Burgundy, when she married the first Lord Haswell. We can scatter a few across our bedroom floors for good measure."

"I doubt we are likely to be attacked," I said. "We are so wholly unconnected to these murders."

But Poppy continued to enumerate the weapons in the house, undeterred: a small cannon in the study, a fanned display of scimitars in the smoking room...

While she cataloged the surprising stockpile of arsenal at Resington Hall—perhaps the gentry had learned its lesson in the civil war—I wondered about the motives of the killer. I could not accept that the actress' death was accidental.

If she was killed, what united these two murders? And was the motive to be found in America?

The field of suspects for the murder of the journalist had been wide open. His criminal activities seemed to have left many people with a reason not to like him, here and in America.

But what was it about the actress that had

prompted her murder? Why was she killed here and why now? Why would the killer wait for her to come to England in order to kill her? Was the killer an Englishman? My thoughts jumped to James, but I did not allow them to go further.

If the actress had done something in the past, in America, in Hollywood, why was it of any concern to anyone here in the Kentish countryside?

No, that couldn't be right. It wasn't just anyone. The killer was most likely someone in the house. Had Ruby been killed because she'd seen who had killed the journalist?

I cast my thoughts back over all the conversations of the preceding days where the actress had participated, searching for a clue in what she'd said that might indicate why she was murdered. But all she had talked about was love and friendship and matters of the heart.

Another idea presented itself. What if she had committed suicide? But why had she chosen to do it here, in England, just before her best friend's wedding? What was it that she had been trying to keep secret?

And while love might have been at the core of Ruby's death, it seemed an unlikely cause for the journalist's demise. Blackmail, theft and a purported murder in America looked to be more fitting causes for his untimely end.

What about Daphne? I mused for a moment.

Could she have killed her friend?

Daphne had sounded rather distressed about the secret the two friends had shared. Had Daphne killed Ruby in order to keep a secret from coming out? Had the actress inadvertently let something slip while drunk? Was Ruby killed because she was an unreliable keeper of Daphne's secret?

I took a pause. I knew so little about Ruby and Daphne and their past. But with the little information I had, it was difficult to see who else in the house, besides Daphne, could have had a motive to kill the actress.

Unless all of this had to do with the Haswells' missing antiques, I conceded.

"And there is something else, Gassy," Poppy said in an ominous tone. I'd forgotten she was walking beside me. Startled out of my thoughts, for a moment I thought someone had found my father's cross. "You better sit down for this," she was saying as she pushed me down on a stone bench. "Since it looks like the actress drowned herself, he seems to be clear of that death at least...but someone has told the police that they saw James walking away from the body of the dead journalist."

"What?!" I exclaimed. "Who?"

"I don't know," Poppy said. "I was as surprised as you are."

I wanted to say it was a lie, but I knew it wasn't. I only wondered why, if someone had spied James, they had waited until this moment to reveal it.

"But don't worry," she added, "he hasn't been arrested yet."

CHAPTER 19

I considered Poppy's information carefully. What did the witness have to gain by this abrupt disclosure? Was it the killer trying to divert attention from himself? And if the killer had observed James in the gardens that day, had he also seen my uncle drifting about?

The thought unsettled me. Now, I was not only worried about James but also concerned for Uncle Albert's safety. What if the killer suspected that he knew more than he did? Would the killer have a go at my uncle?

Then an uncharitable thought popped up in my head. Could Uncle Albert be the one who'd betrayed James? Of course, my uncle would never do such a thing on purpose, but he was not a prize-winning marrow when it came to keeping secrets. He'd proven more than once that his mind was prone to the occasional stumble.

This affair was no longer simply some misunderstanding between Ruby and the journalist. It threatened the very people I cared for deeply. I had to act, for both James' and my uncle's sakes, and I knew exactly where to start.

The Haswells' butler showed me to Daphne's room. I knocked softly on the door, and what sounded like faint sobs coming from the inside stopped.

Daphne opened the door. Her eyes were rimmed with red and red blotches covered her face.

"Yes, what is it?" she asked when she saw me.

"May I come in?"

Daphne regarded me for a moment, then stepped aside to let me in.

She dabbed her eyes as she walked towards the desk by the window and sat down. As she didn't invite me to sit, I remained standing, facing her.

"So, what do you want?" she asked in a curt manner.

I was taken aback by the hostility. "Um, I wanted to offer my condolences. I understand Ruby was a close friend."

"Yes, she was going to be my bridesmaid," Daphne answered and looked away, her gaze traveling to the view out of the window.

I studied her profile and wondered how to proceed. Usually, I was quite adept at making chums with girls. But the fact that she was to be James' bride prevented me from knowing where to start.

"I wanted to talk to you about her death," I said.

She turned around sharply. "Why?" Her dark

eyes bored into me. I could feel she wished me miles away.

"Don't you find your friend's death strange?" I asked.

She shrugged. "What are you, the police?" she scoffed.

"No..." I faltered.

Up close, Daphne was not as nice as she'd appeared on the first evening. She was still dressed nicely, but there was a certain meanness about her—a tightness around the eyes and mouth. She found it difficult to disguise her dislike of me, or perhaps she wasn't even trying. Had she guessed my feelings for James? I pushed that thought away.

"Get on with it," she said, "so I can get on with my day."

Normally, my title and social standing predisposed people towards me, but Daphne seemed to be going out of her way to be impolite. I was finding conversation with her fairly difficult.

"The reason I'm here is because I don't think Ruby's death was an accident," I said.

"And what do you know about it?" she asked. "Did you push her in?"

"No. Of course not!" I said, appalled at the suggestion.

"Did you see who did?" she countered.

"No," I answered, trying to contain my annoyance.

She was goading me, trying to get a rise out of me. If that's how she wanted us to go about it, I would oblige her.

I raised my chin haughtily and adopted the patronizing tone I'd heard my mother use to cower the populace of our parish into doing her bidding. "I overheard you talking to her yesterday at the window," I said, taunting her with an arched eyebrow.

Her countenance changed for a moment, as though a dark cloud passed over her face. But she recovered herself quickly. I wondered if it had been wise for me to admit to her I'd overheard her in the garden. But since James had been implicated, I could see no other way to help him than to get at the truth of these deaths.

"Are you here to blackmail me?" she scoffed again.

"No," I said.

"Then what do you want?" she asked.

"I want to understand what's going on. Two people have died," I said.

"Have you told the police about it?"

"About what? Your conversation? No," I answered. *But I might just do that,* I thought. Or at least threaten Daphne with it, if she didn't start playing along.

Daphne leaned back in the chair as though relenting for a moment. "This is such a ridiculous country," she said, gazing out of the window.

"Everything is old and everyone is so stuffy. I don't know why my dad is so in love with this place. Even my brother is all excited that I'll be marrying into the aristocracy...All I see is ugly houses and ugly men."

"You can't judge the whole country based on this house and Leopold's looks," I said.

Daphne looked up at me and smirked. She got up and went to her purse on the bedside table, and fished out a cigarette case. "Do you want one?" she said, offering me a cigarette.

I shook my head.

She walked over to the window and lit her cigarette. "So what did you hear?" she asked after blowing out her smoke through the crack of the opened window. She turned her dark eyes back to me, but this time the tension in her face had eased.

I wondered where to start. "Ruby wanted you to tell the truth about the brooch the police found. What truth?"

She hesitated before replying. "It got stolen."

I started. *Yet another valuable, pilfered from the house.*

"When?"

"I'm not sure."

"Do you think the journalist stole it?"

She shrugged. "I don't know."

Why would a journalist steal a brooch? Or had someone else taken it and given it to him? But why?

"Was it very valuable?" I asked.

She shrugged again. "I guess. A gift to Ruby from some Hollywood producer."

"But why did she want *you* to talk to the police about it?"

She gazed out of the window, as though arranging her thoughts, before answering. "Because...the brooch was stolen from my room," she said.

"From your room? But I thought the brooch belonged to Ruby?"

"Yes, it belonged to her. But she'd lent it to me to wear. And then it disappeared from my room."

"Why didn't you tell anyone it was stolen?"

"At the time, it didn't matter. There were so many other things going on, the engagement party, and all."

I nodded.

"But I've told the police now," she added.

"And how did it end up with the journalist?"

"I don't know."

The conversation was not proving to be as productive as I'd hoped.

"I heard the dead man, the journalist, was not a nice man," I said, changing direction. "Apparently, he'd been known to resort to blackmail whenever he uncovered anything particularly scandalous."

"Where did you hear that?" Daphne asked

pointedly.

I shrugged and waved a hand to indicate it was a well-known fact. "Was he blackmailing Ruby?" I asked.

"What gave you that idea?"

"Her brooch was in his room and she'd had a meeting with him at the pub," I said.

Daphne did not reply.

"But there's something else," I said, trying to recollect the conversation I'd overheard. "Ruby mentioned that 'the rest' didn't matter now that the journalist was dead. What was 'the rest'?"

Daphne scrutinized me for a moment. "It was just some Hollywood gossip. Ruby was mixed up with someone married. She was desperate for it not to come out."

"Was he the one who gave her the brooch?"

"I guess."

I cast my thoughts back to the day in the garden. Something was not ringing true. "But if the story was about Ruby," I said, "why were you so worried that the story would come out?"

"I'm surprised you remember all of that. I can't even remember what I said that day. I guess I was upset. My parents are forcing me to marry..."

"You don't have to do it," I said.

"You don't know my parents. And anyway, James seems like a nice guy. We'll make it work. I suppose I have to marry someone. And at least

James doesn't talk about money as much as some of the men in New York."

I pushed the thoughts of James away. Was Daphne trying to distract me? I closed my eyes for a moment and strained to remember the exact words between Ruby and Daphne. But I couldn't recall the conversation word for word. All I could recollect was that there was the discussion of the brooch and the impression that Daphne was really upset that someone would discover the truth. There'd been fear in her voice.

"Daphne," I pressed, "I remember you were quite upset that someone would discover the truth, and you wanted Ruby to keep it secret. She said she was always made out to be the bad guy," I said triumphantly, having recalled at least some of the conversation.

"Of course I was upset," she lashed out. "Listen, I don't know why I'm telling you this…you can't tell anyone, okay?" I nodded. "When Ruby was younger," she continued, "she got herself…found herself in trouble, you know? They married, but then he died in the war."

"And the child?"

She gave me a look that made me understand that I should not ask such questions.

"My parents loved Ruby and were very protective of her. Do you know how angry they'd be with me if they knew I'd let some guy get her in trouble?"

I could not understand how Daphne had been meant to protect her friend, but didn't voice my objection.

"And especially now that her Hollywood career was about to take off...it would've ruined her...if any of it came out," Daphne added.

I didn't know enough about Hollywood and how it functioned, but it sounded plausible. Poor Ruby.

"And how did the journalist find out about it?" I asked.

"I don't know. You said he was good at digging up dirt on people," Daphne said and stubbed out her cigarette on the stone sill of the window. "Sorry, do you mind?" She got up and moved towards the door, indicating that our interview was over. "I want to be on my own. Ruby's death has hit me hard."

As I left Daphne and walked down the corridor to my room, I felt uneasy. Although Daphne had answered all my questions and explained everything I'd overheard, something did not sound quite right. I just couldn't be certain what it was that was troubling me.

CHAPTER 20

I feigned a headache and remained in my room during the evening and dinner. I wanted to go over all I had learned so far.

Before Ruby's death, I had suspected her of being the killer. She'd had a strong motive. She'd had a secret. It had all made sense—she had met the journalist in the pub and given him a brooch as payment to keep her secret from coming out.

And what a secret it was! She'd been married young and had had a child. No wonder she wanted to keep it all quiet. But where was that child now?

Had Ruby taken her own life? Had she been unable to live with herself after murdering the journalist?

What if she hadn't killed herself? What if someone had pushed her into the pool? Drunk as she'd been, she had drowned.

If Ruby was murdered, that meant that someone in the house had been worried about her secret coming out? Why?

My mind drifted to my conversation with Daphne. It somehow did not explain Daphne's own involvement in this matter. Would Daphne's own life really have been ruined if Ruby's secret had come out?

Thinking back to the day in the garden, it was Daphne who had sounded really worried. Ruby had only been upset that she was the police's most likely suspect.

What had worried Daphne so much? And had she been the one to push her friend into the pool?

It was an interesting theory. It would also explain why the killer, supposing for a moment it was Daphne, had chosen to kill Ruby despite her being the police's chief suspect. Ruby's usefulness as a scapegoat was outweighed by her propensity for drinking too much. The killer had seen Ruby as a liability. There was something Ruby had known, or had seen, that had made her inconvenient to the killer.

I considered Daphne as a suspect for a moment. Although she could have murdered Ruby, I knew for a fact that she could not have murdered the journalist. According to Poppy, after Daphne broke off her engagement the morning of the murder, she remained in her room the whole day. And with Mrs. Carter, and the servants, going in and out of her room, conducting negotiations with Lady Haswell, Daphne's absence would have been noticed.

Unless, I mused, *Mrs. Carter and Daphne were in this together.* What if Mrs. Carter had only pretended Daphne was in her room, while in fact Daphne had slipped out to kill the journalist?

My mind turned to the dead journalist himself. He had been a crook and a blackmailer. Was it possible that he had been blackmailing other people in the house?

That was one explanation for the missing antiques. Had one of the Haswells used them to pay off the journalist? That thought, unfortunately, brought me back to James. Had he met with the journalist because the Haswells were being blackmailed?

But then, why would James tell the vicar about the missing antiques? Surely, if he was involved in a blackmail payout, he would have kept quiet about the stolen silver. At least that thought gave me some reprieve.

I really needed to talk to James about having seen him on the path. Now that someone else had denounced him to the police, I needed to understand his involvement in this affair. If I knew the truth, perhaps I might be able to help him.

I willed myself to stop thinking about James, and returned to thinking about what connected the journalist and Ruby.

Apart from blackmail, there was also the peculiarity of the dead journalist being afraid to go back to America. Why? Had he really killed someone? Perhaps Ruby's husband had not died in the war. Perhaps the journalist had killed him. It was an interesting thought.

Or had the journalist possessed compromising information about someone in America? Had he tried to blackmail someone powerful in America and it had backfired? Could that someone have been Mr. Carter?

Yes, Mr. Carter looked like the type, I conceded. He had a shady background and uncertain business ventures. No one was quite sure how he had made his money. Perhaps the dead journalist knew something about Mr. Carter's past and was blackmailing him.

It all fit terribly neatly together. Mr. Carter was a smoker. Perhaps it was his cigarettes my uncle had smelled. Perhaps it was him my uncle had seen walking in the distance. And it also explained why Mr. Carter had observed my uncle on the grounds of Resington Hall.

What's more, there had been something disagreeable about the relationship between Ruby and Mr. Carter. She had been far too intimate in her behavior towards him. Were they having an affair?

Ruby's unguarded conduct had perhaps been a hindrance to Mr. Carter's and his political career. Had the journalist been blackmailing Mr. Carter over his affair with Ruby? And had Mr. Carter then murdered Ruby to stop her from revealing it?

What if Daphne had lied to me, or at least had not told me the whole truth? What if she'd known about the relationship between Ruby and her father? What if the brooch had not been a gift from a Hollywood producer but from Mr. Carter?

That would explain why Daphne had been so reluctant to talk to the police about it. It would also explain why she had been so worried when Ruby had asked her to tell the police the truth. She had been worried that the affair would ruin her engagement, the upcoming wedding, and her father's political career.

As Daphne had been quite hostile to me, I did not think she would welcome any more questions from me. And I could certainly not approach Mr. Carter.

I could perhaps go to James and lay out all the facts in front of him and ask his opinion. He was the police's current top suspect, and the one most affected by the resolution of these murders.

Yes, I absolutely needed to speak to James, and tomorrow I would find a way.

But I was beginning to suspect that although these murders took place in England, the motivations for them would be found in America. It was time to reach out to my contacts across the pond.

I could not ask my grandfather for assistance. He would not only worry that I was entangled in a murder, but he would also be concerned that I was associating socially with someone like Mr. Carter. Rather than helping me with retrieving facts about Ruby and the Carters, my grandfather would surely put a stop to my involvement in the matter. But as James' wellbeing—and perhaps Uncle Albert's as well—was at stake, I could not allow that to happen.

It was far safer to involve someone my age. Luckily, I had two cousins my age in America. One was a lawyer in Boston and a bit stuffy. But the other was my cousin Edith, who was currently studying at Barnard College in New York. I knew she would not begrudge me a bit of sleuthing, and would not relate any of it to my grandfather.

Early in the morning, before breakfast, I hopped into my car. Waving to the constable stationed at the gates, I turned towards the village. But I drove past it, and past Canterbury, and proceeded all the way to Dover. I would have preferred to drive to London instead, but that was much too far to drive before breakfast. The distance was necessary, because I feared that any postmistress in a village in the vicinity of Resington Hall was bound to take great interest in my telegram to New York. I sincerely hoped Dover would be far enough.

In the post office, I dispatched a telegram to my cousin. I informed Edith briefly about matters at Resington Hall and begged her discretion. I further asked her to look into Ruby Wilson's marriage in the New York City records. Who had been her husband? And why was the marriage considered so scandalous that it had allowed the journalist to blackmail her, and had perhaps caused her death? Furthermore, I asked her to look into Mr. Carter's affairs and see if anything could shed light on why he might want to murder a journalist and Ruby. Lastly, I asked her to look into the background of the dead journalist, Lance Bradford, and his time in New York. Had he really been implicated in murder?

It was with an easy heart that I drove back to Resington Hall. Things were beginning to fall into place. The matter would soon be resolved, and the specter of suspicion that lay over James would lift.

CHAPTER 21

I arrived back at Resington Hall just in time for breakfast.

Clearing the last bend of the driveway, I spied the vicar coming out of the house. Something in his demeanor caught my attention. He looked as though he was trying to slip out of the house undetected.

He scurried down the stairs and made for a waiting car, with the Haswells' chauffeur standing by.

The vicar gave a little start when he saw me pull up behind the Haswells' car and dropped his Homburg. He nodded in my direction, but got into the waiting car before I had time to get out of mine.

As the chauffeur drove away, the vicar cast a parting glance towards one of the upstairs windows overlooking the driveway. I followed his glance. Lady Haswell was watching the vicar's progress with a drawn face, but she removed herself from the window the moment she caught me looking at her.

I wondered what it all meant.

"Ah, Lady Caroline," Mrs. Carter said as I walked in, "there you are. We were beginning to wonder where all of our English friends were hiding. We thought we got the time for breakfast mixed up," she said with a chortle.

I knew where the vicar and Lady Haswell were, I reflected. But as I looked down the breakfast table, I noticed that the only representative of the Haswell family was James. Poppy had not arrived yet either.

"How about you join my Jack for a game of tennis today, Lady Caroline?" Mrs. Carter continued. "The poor boy hasn't had a chance to play since arriving, and he's very good. He's one of the best tennis players at Princeton. Isn't that right?" She turned and beamed at him. He responded by turning red. "And now that Daphne is part of Lord Haswell's family, it would be nice for Jack to have a lady friend of class to spend time with," she added.

Out of the corner of my eye, I thought I saw James flinch. But what did it matter to him who I played tennis with? He was marrying Daphne.

I tried to hide my smile. Mrs. Carter did not prevaricate. She was intent on getting the most out of her trip across the Atlantic. It would be quite a boon for her if she returned to America with two children betrothed to the British aristocracy.

I eyed Jack. He was indeed quite handsome, in a boyish way. Out of his dinner jacket, he was dressed in the unmistakable Princeton getup —corduroy slacks, and a tennis vest. A cousin of mine had gone to Princeton and had educated me on the style of the university when I had laughed at his incongruous ensemble. According to him, the so-called sport-casual look originated in Princeton and was adopted by all other American universities.

And despite his mother's heavy-handed attempt to pair us up, I wasn't opposed to a game of tennis. Now that James was off limits, I would not mind spending some time in the company of a handsome man.

Plus, the recent deaths had heightened the oppressive ambiance of Resington Hall, and I didn't want to spend the whole day locked up inside this gothic monstrosity. Short of perhaps a visit to Uncle Albert, I had nothing else planned for the day.

"Of course. I'd love to join Jack in a game of tennis," I replied and went to the sideboard to serve myself.

On reflection, perhaps Jack deserved a little diversion. He seemed to be holding up pretty well, but I was convinced that Ruby's death had affected him greatly. Perhaps he didn't want to reveal his true feelings in front of his mother.

Just then, Poppy barged in, pushing the door forcefully. Her outfit left little to the imagination. If the country tweeds and sturdy walking shoes failed to give one the exact idea of where she had been, and what she had been doing, then my uncle's binoculars hanging from her neck galvanized one's suspicions. The fact that Leopold stumbled in right behind her, looking foggy and blushing slightly, told one that they had spent the early hours of the morning, before anyone else had risen, looking at the infernal bird nesting in the forest.

I tried to catch James' eye and share the joke, but he was looking resolutely at the kippers on his plate.

"I'm sorry for your friend's death," I said to Jack.

We had taken a break from our game and were sitting under the umbrella by the tennis court, sipping lemonade. It was another glorious, sunny day. The pool was visible from here. I shuddered. Jack followed my gaze.

"I loved Ruby like a sister, but she was always closer friends with Daphne. Maybe you know how it is, if you have a younger brother?" he asked.

I nodded, but was surprised by his revelation. Could I have misinterpreted his feelings towards

Ruby?

"I know how it is," I said and smiled. "I have a younger brother. He would always sneak around and follow us, but we never wanted him there."

He smiled back. I wondered if he'd known about Ruby's secret marriage.

A devious idea formed in my mind as I sipped my lemonade. Perhaps it had been there from the moment I accepted the game of tennis. I was well aware that I could get some more information about Ruby from Jack. I was particularly interested in her relationship with his father, but I had to go cautiously about it.

"You cared about her a great deal, I think," I said.

Something akin to surprise passed over his face, but he regained his countenance quickly.

"Ruby was a very sweet girl," he said. It was a funny way for a younger man to speak about an older woman, even if the difference in their ages was not that great. "But she needed looking after," he added. "Especially when she'd been drinking."

"I understand perfectly. I have such friends," I said, and gave him a bittersweet smile. "Ruby's death must be terribly hard on your sister," I added after a pause.

"This entire trip is not turning out exactly as we'd hoped," he said.

Yes, I conceded, instead of a future Earl, she'd had to settle for the 4th son of an Earl. A small spark of hope flared up inside me. "Is the wedding going to go forward after all that has happened?" I asked.

He looked surprised. "Yes, of course. Why shouldn't it?"

"Nothing," I said, shaking my head, the spark fizzling out.

"Tell me about Ruby. If you don't mind, of course." He indicated he didn't. "She must have been rather talented to make it in Hollywood," I said.

"The camera loved her, as they say. As far as talent, I'm not a good judge. She wasn't a star yet, but was working her way up. Many of my friends at Princeton were envious that I'd known her since I was a kid."

"What was she like away from the camera and Hollywood? I always picture actors as taking on a persona for the public and being completely different people in their private lives," I said.

"Always sweet. She was pretty much what you saw—fun-loving and vivacious. Perhaps she was a little too interested in getting the attention of men, always talking about love, as you'd probably noticed. But she was devoted to my sister. Her family life had been difficult, and she spent most of her time with my family."

He took a pause, as though deliberating over something. "I'm not ashamed to say that my family had humble beginnings," he continued.

"But with hard work, my father became very successful in his business. His success has allowed me to go to all the right schools, and now my sister is to marry into the English aristocracy." He threw me a sideways glance. "I'm proud of what we have achieved. It's the real American Dream."

I nodded. I was unsure how to proceed now that we'd moved past Ruby and how to bring the conversation back to her relationship with his father. "Do you plan to go into politics, like your father, after Princeton?" I asked.

"I do hope to go into politics, eventually. I'm a member of Whig-Clio at Princeton, and while I plan on a law career, I hope to play a significant role in politics as well."

I nodded again. While I was a bit hazy about American universities, I'd heard of the Whig-Clio debate society from my cousin. Although from humble beginnings, it seemed Jack was an ambitious young man.

"I have an American grandfather, and mother, as you know," I said. "I've always admired that people in America can pursue the American Dream." After a pause, I moved the conversation back to Ruby. "What about Ruby's family? What happened to them?"

"Her father was my father's business partner early on. But her father died. My father did what he could for her, her mother and her siblings."

"Yes, I did get the impression that your father

treated her as one of the family. That's terribly kind of him," I said, trying to sound casual.

He observed me for a few moments with his clear, boyish eyes. "Yes, my father did what he could for her. It was the right thing to do, seeing how she didn't have her father to help her along. My father paid for her trip to Los Angeles and connected her with the right people there."

I wondered if Jack was glossing over some important points in the relationship between Ruby and his father. Was there perhaps something else, some other reason, why Mr. Carter had been so keen on sending her to Hollywood?

But perhaps I was being too cynical. She was the daughter of Mr. Carter's business partner, after all. There needn't have been a sinister reason behind Mr. Carter's desire to help Ruby's career along.

"I'm surprised how small the engagement party is," Jack said, changing tack.

I chuckled. "Yes, I wish there were a few more young people at the party."

I'd wondered about the size of the party as well. It was as though the Haswells were trying to keep most of their acquaintances away from the Americans. Or perhaps, given Lord Haswell's financial difficulties, they were economizing.

"Are you a particular friend of the family?" Jack asked.

"My older brother, Charles, and James were

great friends. My brother died in the war. I'd known James my whole life. Like you and Ruby," I said before thinking.

"Oh, now I understand. I'd wondered about your relationship with James," he said.

I turned to look at him and smiled, to give him the impression that he'd read too much into my relationship with James.

"I hope my sister can count on you as one of her friends after the wedding. You can facilitate her way into society," he said.

The suggestion took me by surprise. Daphne had not been the least interested in my friendship. But I nodded and smiled.

He rose. "Thank you for the game of tennis. It was a pleasure. Perhaps, once my sister is married and my father has purchased Resington Hall, we'll get the opportunity to spend more time together."

Indeed, he was an awfully ambitious young man, I mused. He would make it far in politics.

He bowed slightly, and, relieving me of my tennis racket, offered to walk me back to the house. I considered that I would not mind playing tennis with him again. He was rather good.

But as we walked down the lawn towards the formal gardens, something caught my attention at the edge of the woods. I made a quick, feeble excuse involving Uncle Albert and slipped away.

CHAPTER 22

The movement I'd noticed was that of two figures with binoculars slipping into the woods.

It was the two American ladies—Mrs. Brown and Mrs. Green. If they were frauds, like my uncle insisted, and were not there to watch birds, what were they doing in the forest? Who were they watching?

I plunged into the woods after the ladies.

The dappled green shade of the forest felt cool on my skin after the tennis game. I walked down the path, threading through the trees, and kept an eye out for the ladies among the black trunks. For a moment I stopped to listen for any movement around me, employing all the techniques handed down to me by Frau Baumgartnerhoff. If the two women were anywhere in the forest, I would soon catch them.

"You better come with us, Lady Caroline," said a stern American voice behind me. I jumped around, startled. This was the second time someone had snuck up on me undetected. Were my skills truly diminishing?

Standing in front of me were the two middle-aged Americans. I frowned at them. Who were these women? *And had they just ordered me to come with them?*

"Come with you?" I asked, bewildered. "Where?"

They scowled back and just pointed for me to walk further into the forest. They walked behind me.

As I trudged forward, my thoughts began to race. Something was not quite right here. What did they want with me?

Did they want to show me something they had discovered in the forest? Or was something more sinister going on? For a brief moment, I worried that Uncle Albert had met with an accident snooping on the blasted marrows. Or perhaps Poppy, having finally made use of the binoculars I'd given her, had hurt herself and Leopold was too feeble to help her out.

I turned around with a questioning look, but the women just urged me to keep walking forward.

A branch cracked under my foot and echoed all around the forest. Suddenly, a fear for my own safety gripped me. My thoughts turned more menacing. I hoped Jack had seen me go into the forest, and would come looking for me when my absence was noticed at dinner. But by then, it would probably be too late.

I stumbled over a root, and my dress caught in

the deformed branches jutting out all around me. I wondered if I should yell for help. Perhaps Leopold or Poppy had made their way back to the forest and would hear me. I glanced furtively about, calculating my chances of running away from the two ladies. I was half their age, but there were two of them. And they looked quite sprightly for their age.

As we walked further along, I could feel the silence of the forest pressing on all sides. Here, one could not even hear the birds sing.

If only I had a walking stick, I could do some damage to the two women. But I could not discount the possibility that they might have a gun.

What was concealed at Resington Hall, I mused, that generated so much interest in these two crooks? Was there something specifically valuable hidden there?

"You're not here on a brass-rubbing holiday, are you?" I heard the words roll out of my mouth before I could stop myself. Was it the unbearable stillness of the forest, or was it nerves that compelled me to speak? Perhaps it was my traitorous brain that was always looking to solve puzzles. Or was it the thought that this could be the last human contact I would ever have? I shuddered.

"No, we're not," answered one of them, but did not elaborate.

"What do you think, Dora, is this a good place?" said the other one in a clipped manner that did not allay any of my worries.

"Yes. This is a good spot," the one called Dora answered. "We're unlikely to be overheard this deep in the forest. And if anyone gets near, we'll be able to hear them approach before they see us. You can stop here, Lady Caroline," she commanded me.

I stopped and turned around. The two women stood shoulder to shoulder in front of me. Gone were the feigned smiles of yesterday. Only their steely gazes remained.

I looked around for a sturdy stick, but there was none within arm's reach. I wondered how this was going to play out.

"You are probably wondering why we've brought you out here?" the one whose voice I'd come to associate with Dora spoke up.

I nodded, my throat too dry to speak.

But my brain interrupted to say that one knew perfectly well why they had brought me here, and I did not like the image it conjured up. It further rebuked me for giving into my baser instincts and insisted that what one really wanted to know was who these women were and whether they were spying on someone at Resington Hall.

"We're not on a brass-rubbing holiday, as you've already guessed," said the other one, who wasn't Dora.

Time seemed to stretch, and it offered me

the luxury of examining the two women more closely. Though at first they had appeared so similar to each other, I could now detect slight differences. The one that the vicar had introduced as Mrs. Brown wore green tweeds and was slightly shorter, plumper and with a more kindly look on her face. The other, Mrs. Green, also known as Dora, wore brown tweeds. I mused at the incongruity of it for a moment. Were the names and clothes some sort of strategy to confuse people?

Mrs. Green was slightly taller, with pinched-in cheeks and a stern gaze. She addressed me now. "Have you guessed what we've been doing in the forest, Lady Caroline?" she asked.

Planning a heist, I wanted to say, but restrained myself.

"Your uncle tells us you are quite good at figuring out puzzles," she continued.

Uncle Albert! Guaranteed to say the wrong thing to the wrong people! Why would he boast about my abilities to women he suspected of being criminals? Or was it his way of warning them off?

"Have you perhaps figured out why we are watching the big house?" she added, referring to Resington Hall, I assumed.

I shook my head. I wanted to say that I suspected them of being thieves and somehow connected to the Rev. Quinton in Canterbury and the murders at Resington Hall, but of course did not vocalize these musings.

"Before we tell you our reason for being here," Mrs. Green said, "let me ask you this, do you know who is in that fancy mansion at the moment?"

I shrugged. "Lord and Lady Haswell," I hazarded a guess.

Mrs. Green examined me for a moment as though trying to figure out if I was being facetious. "What do you know about the Americans who are currently visiting Lord and Lady Haswell?" she asked.

What was going on here? What were they implying with all these questions about Resington Hall?

And why were they engaging in conversation if they were about to bump me off? But as I was quite curious to see where they were going with their query, I played along.

"Not much. Their daughter is engaged to be married to one of Lord Haswell's sons." I could not bring myself to say his name.

"And do you know anything about Mr. Carter himself?" Mrs. Brown asked.

I shrugged. "He's a businessman. According to my mother, he is quite well off, but the exact nature of his business is unclear," I said.

As they seemed to know more about this whole affair, I wondered why they were posing all these questions to me.

"How well does your mother know Mr. Carter?" Mrs. Green asked with malice in her voice.

Tension gripped the space between my shoulder blades. Why were they asking me about my mother? "I do not think she knows him well at all," I said, bristling on her behalf. "She was quite incensed that the Haswells had sprung the Carters up on her, as she put it."

The two women studied me for a moment as though determining how to proceed.

I gazed back at them. This charade had gone on long enough. It was time to resolve this whole affair. "Why have you brought me out here, in the middle of the forest?" I asked with suspicion.

"To talk to you, dear, of course," said Mrs. Brown in a kindly voice.

"But why me?" I asked, exasperated. It was clear these ladies did not have murder on their mind. They were after something else entirely. "What is the information you imagine I possess? I don't know anything about Mr. Carter, and neither does my mother." I started to leave.

"Not so fast, Lady Caroline," Mrs. Green said and raised her hand to bar my way. "We do have a point here."

"We've been watching the Haswells, and your family, ever since Mr. Carter arrived in England," Mrs. Brown said.

That declaration made me halt, indeed.

CHAPTER 23

The women's admission shocked me. Why had they been watching my family?!

I glared at them. Who were these women? They sounded more and more ridiculous by the minute.

"And why would two American women be watching two respectable English families?" I asked, indulging them in their little game.

"You could say we've been doing it for your safety," Mrs. Green said. "Mr. Carter may be a very wealthy man now, but he made his money in some very shady ways."

"Racketeering was the nicest part of his business," added Mrs. Brown.

"But he has since retired and has decided to enter politics," Mrs. Green said, taking over. "He's been making friends with all the right people and making donations to all the right places."

"Whitewashing his past, so no one would ask uncomfortable questions," Mrs. Brown elaborated.

"Are you telling me he's a gangster?" I asked, incredulous. Though, upon reflection, I was not surprised by the revelation.

"To an extent," Mrs. Green said. "Though, as we said, he's retired." She gave me a look that said she expected me to keep up.

"Is he wanted by the police?" I asked.

How could the Haswells have entangled themselves with such a man? Perhaps Lord Haswell's poor judgment had brought more than financial destitution upon his family. I wondered for a moment if Lady Haswell had guessed something of Mr. Carter's past, given her uncharitable glances towards her own husband.

"He's not wanted by the police," Mrs. Green interrupted my thoughts. "How he made his money is of no concern to the government."

"But the United States Treasury is concerned that he has been hiding his money and not paying the government its dues," added Mrs. Brown. "Tax evasion," she clarified.

I nodded. I was well aware of the crippling effect of government taxes. They were the undoing of more than one noble British family.

"So, what is your role in all of this?" I asked, still unclear about who these women were, uncertain about how what they were telling me had any bearing on me, and surprised that they were making these revelations to me at all.

"We are undercover agents of the United States government," Mrs. Brown said.

The assertion almost made me laugh, but I contained my astonishment. Was this some sort of trick? These ladies did not strike me as government agents.

"We suspect that Mr. Carter is exploring new ventures to conceal his wealth from the government, and that his foray into England is some sort of scheme to establish connections in this country and enter into shady deals," Mrs. Green said. "Why would he want his beloved daughter to marry into the family of an impoverished Lord, if not for the connections such an alliance would bring him?"

There was some plausibility to this. Despite his financial failings, Lord Haswell was quite well connected in government and business.

"There need not be any sinister forethought," I countered, thinking of my own parents' union. "A lot of American families marry into the British aristocracy to raise their social standing."

"That is not Mr. Carter's way. We are sure he would try to find a way to use his new connections to his *financial* benefit, not social," Mrs. Green said.

"And to the detriment of the Treasury," Mrs. Brown added.

"And where does my family fit in?" I asked with unease, having not forgotten the women's admission that they had been watching us.

"With your mother being American, we wondered if there was a connection. Your family was one of the first ones the Carters visited when they arrived in England."

"That's why you were at our parish church!" I said. "You were there to spy on the meeting between my family and the Carters." I thought back to all the times the ladies had seemed to pop up, as if by chance. "You were even spying on our vicar in Canterbury, and me, and even my uncle!"

They smiled. "Running into your uncle was a lucky coincidence," Mrs. Brown said.

"But we followed the vicar because when we met him at your parish church, he told us he was planning to carry some very valuable items to Canterbury," Mrs. Green said. "We had to make sure he wasn't involved in some intricate scheme of money laundering and concealment between your mother and Mr. Carter."

"Art is a well-known form of obscuring income," Mrs. Brown added.

"And you suspected I was involved as well, driving the vicar, staying at the Haswells' home," I said.

They nodded.

"But if you suspect me of colluding with Mr. Carter, why are you telling me all this?" Something didn't seem quite right.

"We made some enquiries," Mrs. Green said. "It appears your family, although peculiar in its own ways, is in the clear of any financial cover-ups."

"And is there some kind of art trickery taking place?" I asked, worried, thinking of Rev. Quinton's uneasy presence in Canterbury. My mother would be devastated to know that the family heirlooms could be thus polluted.

"Not that we have been able to detect," Mrs. Green conceded.

"But what about all the antiques that have disappeared from Resington Hall?" I asked. I could have also mentioned my father's cross, but didn't want to muddle the matters.

"We don't think Mr. Carter had any involvement in that," Mrs. Green said. "He hasn't left Resington Hall in the past few days."

"But that doesn't mean that he would not have agents doing his bidding," Mrs. Brown added.

"Why tell me all this?" I asked. "Why not go to the police with the information you have?"

"We are here in an incognito capacity, dear," said Mrs. Brown. "We don't want the British police to suspect our motives. It's best to keep our cover for now."

"Plus, it would be good to have an agent inside the house. Someone who can keep an eye on Mr. Carter up close," said Mrs. Green.

"You mean me?"

They nodded. I shrugged. I was already snooping around anyway.

"And what about the deaths?" I asked.

"The deaths are of no concern to us," said Mrs. Green.

"They were a surprise," said Mrs. Brown, and

her brown eyes grew large.

"Do you think Mr. Carter is behind them?" I asked.

"It's not the way he operates," said Mrs. Green.

"That is to say, he's always had someone else do his dirty work," said Mrs. Brown.

"And these days he keeps his nose clean. Politics and workers' unions are a much better way to make money. He would not jeopardize that golden goose so easily with murder," scoffed Mrs. Green.

"But even if he is involved in murder, that is for the local police to figure out," Mrs. Brown added. "It's of no concern to the United States Treasury. He just needs to pay his taxes."

Mrs. Green nodded her assent.

I considered for a moment the slightly deranged priorities of the two women.

"The day of the murder," I said, remembering suddenly, "you were coming out of these woods, on the other end, by the road. Did you not see anything?"

"Just that nice young man that bird-watches," said Mrs. Brown.

"Leopold?" I asked. The women nodded. This matched my uncle's own observations. "Anyone else?" I pressed.

"His brother walking in the direction where the body was discovered later," Mrs. Green said.

I groaned. "Anyone else?" I asked, but was not

terribly hopeful.

"Your uncle," Mrs. Green answered.

"And no one else?" I asked, the flame of hope slowly dying inside me.

"No, dear," said Mrs. Brown.

Preposterous! I exclaimed in my head.

But something else troubled me. "Why all these dramatics of dragging me into the forest?" I asked.

"You came looking for us, my dear," Mrs. Brown said.

"And we had to make sure our conversation would not be overheard," added Mrs. Green.

"But all this time, you've been so obvious!" I exclaimed. "Everyone has noticed you around. How can you claim you are undercover?"

"The best way to hide is in the open, dear," Mrs. Brown said.

"The quickest way to be spotted is if you try to hide," added Mrs. Green.

"Who would suspect anything unusual about two old ladies on a brass-rubbing holiday?" Mrs. Brown asked rhetorically.

My uncle, for one, I countered in my head.

"You have an inquisitive mind, Lady Caroline," Mrs. Green said. "But it's best not to get tangled up in affairs related to Mr. Carter."

"It's for your own good, dear," Mrs. Brown added.

I was not quite certain if this was meant as

helpful advice or as a warning. I left the women to their espionage and went to think about all the seemingly random facts I had learned.

Although the two American ladies did not believe Mr. Carter was involved, I could not help but think it was no coincidence that all of these incidents—disappearing antiques, deaths— had begun with the arrival of the Carters in England.

What was the connection between the murdered journalist, the dead actress, Mr. Carter's past, and the missing antiques?

As I made my way out of the forest and across the lawns, it occurred to me that the two women had revealed very little about what they had uncovered.

Was Mr. Carter actually in the process of establishing a nefarious network in England? Was Lord Haswell in danger of being made a fool of by an American ex-gangster?

I wondered if Lord Haswell was aware of Mr. Carter's background. Or whether he even cared. For a moment, I contemplated whether the two deaths were connected to Lord Haswell's financial troubles.

But as Lord Haswell's failings were well known, and had been discussed at length in the press, I didn't see how anyone could embarrass him any further so as to drive him to murder. Nothing the journalist or Ruby could have uncovered about him could have brought more damage to Lord Haswell than the damage he had already brought onto himself.

No, the more likely reason for the two deaths lay in Mr. Carter's gangster past, I decided. The Carters were trying to buy their way into nobility. Perhaps, back home, in America, society was acutely aware of their past, and they had come to England to inject some class and respectability into their family.

But even if Mr. Carter was here to evade taxes, as the two American ladies claimed, how was that connected to the two deaths?

CHAPTER 24

As I left the forest, another thought occurred to me, and I had to chuckle. Never once had the government agents mentioned my father. Even to people who had spied on my family only for a day or two, it was clear who wielded the power at our castle.

"Lady Caroline," the Haswells' butler said as I walked into the house, "how fortuitous. I was just coming to look for you. A lady is holding on the telephone for you."

My heart sank. Was it possible that Edith was calling me back already? I tried to do a quick mental calculation of the time difference with New York, but in my distress, my brain failed me. But regardless of what time it was in New York, the few hours that had passed since I had cabled her would not have been sufficient to gather all the information I had inquired about. Perhaps she was calling me to tell me she could not help me. But why not send me a telegram instead of making an expensive telephone call? I wondered.

"Hello?" I said into the handset, "Caroline speaking."

"Caroline," came a voice on the other end that I could not place at the moment, but which sounded quite crisp. The connection with New York was flawless. "It's Louisa," said the voice.

"Louisa!" For an instant I wondered what she was doing calling me, but then I remembered our mutual acquaintance, the luscious-haired reverend. "What news?"

"Well, remember that task you had assigned me?"

"Yes, vividly." My mind jumped to the vicar's odd behavior this morning.

"I have some news on that front. Should I give it to you over the telephone or would you prefer to meet in person?"

I looked around the corridor. It seemed fairly deserted. "Perhaps I can have it now," I said. I'd had enough conferences in person for one day.

"As you wish. Well, I'd been keeping an eye on Rev. Quinton, as you'd asked, and the most curious thing happened this morning. Your vicar came to the Deanery and showed something to Rev. Quinton. It was all very hush-hush. And Rev. Quinton ushered your vicar outside, as though he didn't want them to be observed."

I took a seat on the chair next to the telephone. Was our vicar involved in some sort of smuggling of antiques with Rev. Quinton? The vicar was certainly gullible enough to be embroiled in one of the dashing reverend's schemes.

"Caroline, are you still there?" Louisa asked.

"Yes, I'm still here. Sorry. Please continue."

"I made some excuse to go outside and managed to follow them. They had some quick discussion in the gardens, but then proceeded to leave the Precincts. Your vicar put away whatever it was that he had brought to show Rev. Quinton. He looked like he was hiding it. But I managed to steal a quick peek. It was not a religious item, by the looks of it. It was something silver, smooth and shiny."

"Were you able to follow them further?"

"Yes, I was," Louisa said, and I could hear the smile in her voice. "And I followed them all the way to an antiques shop."

"Really? I hope they didn't see you."

"No, there were enough pilgrims milling about so I could blend in with the crowd. But I didn't follow them into the shop. I waited until they came back out. Whatever your vicar had been carrying, he'd left in the shop. And I saw both men pocket some money. I guess they split the proceeds of whatever they'd sold in the shop. Then Rev. Quinton left to walk back to the Precincts, but your vicar just stood around, looking lost." Yes, that was an apt description of the vicar. "That's when I saw my chance." I could hear her smile again.

"What did you do, Louisa?"

"I ambushed him."

I chuckled. Poor vicar, everyone was quite

quick to take his measure.

"Do you want me to tell you what I found out?"

Just then, I saw the vicar walk in through the front doors. Our eyes met, and he quickly looked away.

"Thank you, Louisa," I said, eager to put the receiver down. "I'll take it from here. Thank you," I added hastily, before disconnecting.

"Ah, Rev. Bamford," Lady Haswell's voice came behind me before I could address the vicar myself. "Just the man I wanted to see."

"I'm sorry, Lady Haswell," I interrupted her, "there is an urgent matter I'd like to discuss with the vicar."

Lady Haswell spared me a withering glance and extended a bony hand towards the vicar, as though to lead him away. "My matter is just as urgent, and as I am the mistress of this house," she said and took a brief pause, as though she wanted to add 'at least for now', "I must insist."

"Rev. Bamford is the vicar of our parish," I insisted in turn. "I received some very distressing news over the telephone just now that I need to discuss with him."

The vicar stood frozen, his gaze switching to and fro, uncertain which way to go.

As I observed Lady Haswell's huffs at my impertinence, my mind jumped to this morning and her odd countenance at seeing the vicar leave in the family car.

"I've just received a call from Canterbury," I said, and Lady Haswell jumped as though stung. "Perhaps we could all talk somewhere privately," I suggested.

"This will do," she said, as she led us into the library. "What is it you wished to say, Lady Caroline?"

"I've become aware that antiques have been disappearing from this house, and this morning, Rev. Bamford was observed going into an antiques purveyor in Canterbury. I suspect he was there to sell an item he took from this house. And I further suspect that it was with your sanction, Lady Haswell."

The vicar was scanning the floor, too embarrassed to look at me. But Lady Haswell remained unmoved by my exposition.

"There is nothing suspicious," she said, head held at an uncomfortably odd angle. "As we don't all have the benefit of an American dowry," she looked pointedly at me, "some of us have to resort to selling family heirlooms to keep afloat. This engagement party has cost us a fortune. And as my husband has so foolishly parted us with our money, the only way to finance this endeavor was to sell a few trinkets. No harm done. Nothing to concern yourself with." She stuck her chin up and regarded me with contempt.

"I understand," I mumbled. I was mortified that I'd forced Lady Haswell to make such an admission in front of me. "But since Rev. Bamford is our parish vicar, I need to understand his role in all this." I turned to look at the vicar, who had gone pale and was perspiring.

Lady Haswell hesitated before answering. "I've been working with an individual in Canterbury, who has superior knowledge of antiques, and who has been helping me select the best items to sell." I knew she was referring to Rev. Quinton, but opted to keep my knowledge of his involvement to myself, lest Louisa's position would be jeopardized. "But with these deaths, and police and journalists about," Lady Haswell continued, "it became quite inconvenient for me to go to Canterbury. I didn't want to be observed. So I sent the vicar." She cast him an icy glance, as though blaming him for the failed mission. "We're cousins," she added with distaste.

I nodded.

"How did you come to hear of it?" Lady Haswell asked.

While trying to come up with a plausible explanation that would not involve Louisa, the door opened.

"Pardon the interruption, Lady Haswell," the butler said upon entering. "The police inspector is here. He's looking for Master James."

Lady Haswell departed abruptly, waving the butler impatiently out of the way. I followed in her wake.

As we walked out of the front doors, we saw James being led away to a waiting police car by a constable.

"No," Lady Haswell cried as she ran after James. She turned to look for the police inspector. "What evidence do you have against him?" she snapped at the hapless official when she located him.

"A note, arranging a meeting with the deceased, Lance Bradford, just prior to the journalist's death," he answered.

The note I'd seen James pick up!

Suddenly, Lady Haswell dissolved into hysterical sobbing. She looked frantically between James and Daphne, who had just come out on the front steps. For a moment I wondered if Lady Haswell was crying because James was being arrested or because the wedding—and with it the sale of Resington Hall, and the promise of Mr. Carter's money—was in jeopardy.

Daphne did not look moved by the scene and gazed cooly on the proceedings. One would think she welcomed these developments.

As the police inspector was still preoccupied with calming Lady Haswell down, I saw my chance. I sprang to James. One of the constables on James' side tried to prevent me from getting close to him, but I gave him a look that said, *do you know who my father is?*, and he cowered back.

James regarded me curiously. I stepped right up to him and made as though to kiss him, but instead, I moved my lips to his ear.

"Tell me about the note," I whispered.

"It wasn't meant for me. Ask Leopold," he answered, his lips brushing my skin. I breathed in his warmth and time stood still.

"That's enough of that, miss." The firm hands of a policeman pulled me away from James.

But I'd received enough to go on.

As I turned around, I scanned the faces of all of those gathered on the steps, gaping at the commotion.

Lady Haswell's face showed pure outrage at my behavior. It said that if the arrest had not jeopardized the engagement, my scandalous behavior certainly had. I cast a quick glance at Daphne. She only smirked back.

Then my eyes latched onto the only person I was interested in at the moment—Leopold.

CHAPTER 25

Perhaps seeing the determination in my eyes, Poppy, who was standing next to Leopold, moved to protect him with her body.

"Step aside, Poppy," I said, not in the least bit intimidated by her at that moment, "I need to speak with Leopold."

"Now, Beastly," she said threateningly, using one of the less flattering sobriquets she had for me, "Leopold has nothing to do with this."

"How do you know?" I countered. But I also failed to see why James had told me to speak to Leopold. What did he have to do with the murders?

I took a pause to compose myself. Everyone gathered on the steps—from Leopold's brothers and their wives to the Carters—was staring at us. I needed to speak to Leopold in private.

"Leopold, please," I addressed him, "can we go to the library, perhaps?" I gave him a pleading look and hoped he would acquiesce. At that moment, I wished I hadn't been so horrid to him so many times when he had offered me marriage. I wondered if he would hold it against me.

Leopold nodded and turned to go back inside. Lady Haswell advanced towards her son as though to go with him. But I glared at her and she relented. She did, however, manage to smooth down a stray lock across his balding forehead.

"I'm coming," Poppy declared.

I nodded. Her presence could not be helped. And perhaps it would be beneficial to have the support of Poppy, although I suspected that she had shifted allegiance over the past few days.

I allowed Leopold to lead the way, as this was his house and he probably knew the rooms better. He led us into a reception room of some kind.

Poppy elected to stand sentinel, in a wide stance, with arms crossed, while I perched on the sofa across from Leopold.

"Leopold," I began, "why was James arrested?"

He glanced at Poppy before answering. She nodded at him. "The police found a note in his possession," he said softly, "from the dead journalist arranging a meeting."

I flinched. I'd never actually heard Leopold's customary voice. Having only ever heard him in the state of groveling, under duress from his mother, when advancing offers of marriage to me, it was strange to hear him speak outside circumstances related to drawing room proposals.

I regained my composure quickly. "Why would this journalist want a meeting with James?"

Leopold squirmed in his seat and glanced at

Poppy again.

"I say! What a bind James finds himself in. Eh, Gassy?" Poppy piped up.

I nodded. Why had James kept this incriminating note? Why hadn't he disposed of it? Silly, honorable, James, I despaired. But there was more to what James had whispered to me.

"Only the note was not for James, was it?" I pressed. "Who was the note for? Was it for you, Leopold?"

He nodded imperceptibly.

"Why you? What did the note say?" I asked.

Leopold cast another quick glance at Poppy.

"Rally round, old bean," she encouraged him, and slapped him heartily on the back. He sputtered and coughed.

"It arranged for a meeting by the gates at two o'clock," Leopold said. "The note said the journalist had some information about my upcoming engagement that I might find to my benefit."

I narrowed my eyes at him. "If the note was for you, why did James go in your place?"

"Well, I showed the note to James, asking him what I should do?"

"Were you suspicious of the man's motives?" I asked.

"No, no, nothing like that. But I usually go to observe the short-toed snake eagle pair nesting in the woods right after lunch. I make my observations early in the morning and right after lunch." He fished a black notebook out of his pocket and leafed through it. "Here are the records of my visits to the nest for the past fortnight." He turned it in my direction so I could see for myself. "I could not miss an observation. It would throw all my sightings data into a disarray." He tapped one of the open pages of his booklet.

Poppy nodded emphatically on Leopold's behalf. "I quite agree. How could one expect Leopold to present his findings at the next meeting of the Canterbury Chapter of the South East England Ornithological Observation and Preservation Club, Kent Division, if he lacks complete records of his sightings? Leopold is hoping to be elected Chapter Secretary within the next three years. I'm quite confident he can make it in two, with my help."

I quite regretted giving Poppy that pair of binoculars at the moment. She was turning into an insufferable twitcher.

"Damn impertinent of this journalist chap to jeopardize your observations, Leopold," she added for good measure.

I couldn't say whether Leopold was qualified to be Chapter Secretary of the South East England Ornithological Observation and Preservation Club, but he was jolly well ready for full membership of Uncle Albert's Royal Society for Natural History Appreciation.

We were, however, slowly drifting away from the point. I took a deep breath. "So James offered to go to the meeting on your behalf?" I asked.

"That's right," Leopold answered, pulling his eyes reluctantly away from the pages of his little book. "He thought the journalist might have something of importance to communicate."

"And do you know if James got to speak to the journalist?"

"No, he said he was dead when he got there. He was walking back to the house to inform everyone. That's when he saw you."

I nodded. "And did you tell the police that?"

"Tell them what?"

"That the note was meant for you, and not James," I said. "And that James discovered the journalist already dead. James would have no reason to kill the journalist."

"They were not quite prepared to believe me, since I am his brother, and since I was actually in the forest at the time and hadn't observed anything of their meeting."

There was no meeting. "Did the note give any indication of what the journalist might have wanted to tell you?" I asked instead.

Leopold shook his head.

"But we can assume it was something about Daphne?" I ventured.

He gave a noncommittal shrug.

"So someone killed the journalist before James got there," I mused out loud. "You didn't happen to see anyone?"

"Well, there were two lady birdwatchers. Quite excited when I told them about my sightings."

Whoever killed the journalist must have known about the meeting, I considered. But how?

"How was the note delivered?" I asked.

"By post," Leopold replied, using a tone that suggested my question was silly.

"So no one would have had a chance to read it before you received it?"

"I should think not!"

"Jolly good. Where were you when you were discussing the note with James?"

"In the morning room."

"Were the doors to the garden open?"

"Perhaps," Leopold said uncertainly. "Yes, they were. I could hear the song of a *Fringilla coelebs* coming in through the open doors. A chaffinch," Leopold clarified, turning to Poppy. "It makes a series of descending notes, called the 'chaffinch's rain song'. It's rather charming and ends with a characteristic 'didioo' twirl. I will indicate it to you next time we hear it."

"Leopold," I interjected. "Do you think someone might have overheard your discussion with James?"

"Oh, yes. It's quite possible. Though I don't

know how anyone could have heard anything over the racket Daphne was making." He shuddered a bit and then gazed lovingly at Poppy.

"Daphne had already started crying by the time you received the note?" I asked, intrigued.

Leopold nodded. "Oh, yes. She initiated proceedings against me first thing that morning. That was another reason why I did not feel in any way obliged to hear what the journalist had to say." He puffed out his chest slightly as though congratulating himself on a decision well made.

The clock chimed. "Sorry, Gassy, old girl," Poppy said and clapped her hands. It was a gesture she had used as Head Girl to indicate that matters were settled and not open to discussion or objections. "We'll have to cut this short. Leo is due for another sighting."

Leo? It looked as though Poppy had discovered a pet project to keep herself occupied. Though the relationship reminded one of an orca whale playing with its prey before eating it. But who was I to judge?

As they left the room, I stayed behind to collect my thoughts. Someone had overheard Leopold and James discussing the note and the meeting time. Someone else had got there before James and done away with the journalist. But who?

And was it not suspicious that Daphne had decided to sabotage the engagement on the very morning that the journalist was to meet with

Leopold and reveal some sort of secret to him? I nodded to myself.

So the journalist was most likely killed to keep him from revealing a secret about Daphne. But why had the journalist been so interested in sharing this secret with Leopold? Was he hoping that Leopold would pay for it? The journalist must have known that the Haswells were in no position to pay for such things.

Was Ruby killed because she had been aware of this secret and was in danger of revealing it? A chill washed over my body. Would Daphne kill her childhood friend?

She couldn't have, I argued with myself. She was crying in her room. Unless, someone else was doing the crying for her. Like her mother.

It was an easy way to provide her with an alibi, I mused.

What was this terrible secret? I wondered as the afternoon slipped away and turned into evening.

"Dear lady, you can't expect my Daphne to marry a murderer," Mr. Carter was saying to Lady Haswell during dinner. "There's nothing I can do about it," he continued. "With your son in jail, there's no one Daphne is interested in marrying now."

Lady Haswell gave a small sob in reply and dabbed at her eyes. She then glared at each of her sons in turn. I could see that she had assisted Leopold with his hair, and had brushed it diligently to the side, over his balding crown, but it did little to improve his appearance, or his appeal to Daphne.

I wondered what her expectations were of her two married sons. Perhaps she hoped they'd renounce their wives and offer themselves to Daphne.

Lady Haswell and my mother were kindred spirits in the amount of disappointment their families furnished them with.

"Our minds are made up," added Mrs. Carter. "We are leaving tomorrow as soon as our luggage gets packed. We'll miss this house, though," she added, as though trying to lessen Lady Haswell's disappointment. "It's so pretty. It's such a shame I won't get to renovate it."

"It is a beautiful house, Barbara," Mr. Carter turned to his wife, "but I'll get you another nice one, maybe in Havana."

Mr. Carter's announcement at the start of dinner that his family was departing tomorrow had sent Lady Haswell into hysterical sobbing. His declaration was the final confirmation that the wedding, and with it any promise of money, was off.

Now that James was charged with the murder

of the journalist, the wedding could not go on.

I sat observing the proceedings in anguish. Although events had played out exactly as I'd wanted—the ghastly Americans were leaving, and James was free of Daphne—somehow now everything was more abysmal than even the evening when Daphne's engagement to James was announced.

One of the Americans, most likely Daphne, was the murderer. And the murderer was about to leave and go back to America, and James would hang for a murder he did not commit.

I considered talking to the police, but the fact that they were letting the Americans leave the country meant that the inspector had made up his mind on the matter. There was little I could do on James' behalf. I had no evidence that any of the Americans had a reason to kill either the journalist or Ruby.

My last hope rested with my cousin in New York.

CHAPTER 26

I walked down to breakfast, even more dejected than the previous night. I didn't even want to go into the breakfast room. I couldn't face the Carters. Or the Haswells.

Loitering in the hallway for a short while, I was indecisive about what to do. A visit to Uncle Albert was perhaps in order. He would not be able to provide any insight, but we could commiserate together.

"Good morning, Lady Caroline," the butler addressed me, as he came out of the breakfast room. "If you are planning to leave before having breakfast, may I bring your attention to a telegram waiting for you?"

"Yes?!" I asked, barely able to contain my excitement.

"I'm afraid the sender from New York got the time difference quite wrong," he continued with a slightly acerbic tone. "I was just making my rounds at around midnight, checking that all the doors and windows were properly locked, when a messenger arrived. But I did not want to trouble you while you were sleeping. I've left it with the rest of the mail in the breakfast room."

I hardly waited for the butler to finish his piece and rushed to the room. Ordinarily I would have expressed my displeasure at the delay in the message's delivery, but at the moment all I cared about was getting to the telegram.

Barging into the breakfast room, I spared a quick 'good morning' for the few that had made it down, and scanned the sideboard for the telegram.

Perhaps sensing the urgency at last, the butler had followed me back into the room, and shuffling through the morning post himself, handed me the telegram envelope.

Electing to read the message in a more private place, I left the breakfast room again, and took the first chair I spied in the hallway.

Ripping the envelope open, I retrieved the message and read.

I took a few shallow breaths. My cousin had used initials to identify the information she had discovered about the Carters. For a moment, the letters just swam before my eyes, and I could not make sense of them.

But my bewilderment lasted only a few moments. I rose abruptly from the chair. The killer and motive had become clear to me.

I ran up the stairs and turned towards the bedrooms. I knew the exact location of the bedroom I was looking for. The butler had shown me to it previously.

I barged in without knocking into Daphne's room.

"How dare you?" she cried out after she had recovered from her initial shock at my entrance. "What are you doing here?" She glared at me.

I had to take a few breaths to calm myself down from running up the stairs, and to quell enough of the anger I felt towards Daphne before I could speak.

"You lied," I panted, unable to wait for my breath to catch up with my thoughts. "You lied to me about Ruby's marriage."

"What are you talking about? Get out of here before I call my father," she threatened.

I waved the telegram. "I have proof," I said and instantly regretted not leaving the telegram somewhere safe. Suddenly realizing the danger I'd put myself in, I purposely remained by the door and propped it open with my foot in case I needed to make my escape.

Daphne's eyes blazed, staring at the telegram. "You little, interfering cow," she spat, but she didn't move towards me. She remained by the trunk she had been packing when I had barged in.

"I have a cousin in New York," I said, undeterred by her insult. "She looked up the New York marriage and birth records." I took a step towards her, then reconsidered my move. "You lied," I repeated. "Ruby was not married. There was no child!" I declared.

"So? That doesn't prove anything. Maybe she was married in another city. Maybe she had the child somewhere else." The look in her eyes challenged me to contradict her.

I couldn't. She was probably right. Ruby could have been married in any other city in America. But that was not the most damning piece of information the telegram contained.

"It would appear that the New York City Clerk's Office keeps terribly detailed records, which list the names and addresses of marriage witnesses." I took a dramatic pause. "Ruby might not have been a bride, but she was a witness to another marriage. Do you want me to tell you whose?" I asked slowly.

The color drained from Daphne's face. Her eyes widened in panic. I wondered if she was about to attack me, and took a preemptive step back.

"Please, don't," she said, and I heard the same fear in her voice as the day I'd overheard her in the garden.

"You were married," I said, unable to stop myself. I had to hear myself say it in order to believe it. "You were married to Lance Bradford, the dead journalist."

"Close the door," she cried and lunged in my direction. I jumped out of her way, but she only reached for the door to close it.

I stood with my back to the wall. My sense for preservation was fighting with my curiosity. I had to know.

"Did you kill him?" I asked, barely breathing out the words.

She shook her head and walked towards her bed.

"Do you know who did?"

"No," she whispered, and sat down on the edge of the mattress. She stared at the floor. Tears began running down her face.

Although she had already lied to me once quite convincingly, I somehow believed that she was telling the truth.

"Tell me about it," I said. "Please. It might help save James."

"I don't see how," she said, and wiped her tears off her face. "But I guess since you know some of it, you might as well know all of it."

I hesitated and then went to sit by her side.

"Lance worked for my father, running errands for him…That's how I met him. There was something dangerous and adventurous about him. He had a British accent. All the girls were crazy about him…I was so young. And in love. And when he suggested we should get married, I was over the moon."

She remained silent for a while.

"That was seven years ago. I was so scared to tell my father. I begged Ruby and Stan, the two witnesses, to keep it secret."

Her hands were trembling in her lap.

"A few days after we were married, Lance came to me and said that he had enlisted in the army. He said he had to go fight for his country. That was towards the end of the war, 1918. And he just left me. And that was the last I heard from him. I thought he died in the war, and since no one knew we were married, no one knew to tell me. And I kept thinking he was dead until we came here."

I nodded.

"My mother was trying to set me up with guys in New York," she continued. "To marry me off. But I kept refusing. I was scared that my marriage to Lance would be discovered. Then, my father decided he wanted to enter politics, and got this idea that I should marry into the English gentry, to raise his profile in society. My mother had read an article about it in a magazine. I could not hold my parents off any longer. They both really liked the idea of being related to aristocrats...And then Ruby found out that if your husband was dead or had not contacted you for seven years, the marriage was annulled. I thought I was in the clear and agreed to marry Leopold. I also liked the idea of being a Lady."

"But Lance was not dead," I added. "And then you arrived in England, and news of your upcoming engagement spread in the press." I was starting to see where Daphne's story was going.

She nodded. "Lance had become a journalist in England after the war, and he'd seen my name in the papers. He contacted me and demanded money. He would keep quiet and pretend he was never married to me if I paid him. I didn't have any money on me, and didn't want to give him anything valuable that belonged to me, in case our connection somehow came out, so I asked Ruby to pay him off for now with the brooch. Ruby told me not to give in to him, that seven years had passed, that it was time to tell my father. But I was so scared of what my parents would say if they found out. I begged her to keep my secret. She met with Lance at the tavern and gave him the brooch."

"And then when he was murdered, it looked as though he had been blackmailing Ruby and she had killed him," I said.

"I was such a coward," she said. "I should have protected Ruby."

"What do you think happened to Ruby? Do you think someone pushed her into the pool on purpose?"

"I don't know. I don't think so. I think it was an accident. Ruby was so nice. No one would have a reason to kill her. Especially here in England. No one knows her here."

"What if she had seen the real killer?" I suggested.

Daphne shook her head. "No. She would have told me. Or the police."

"And the story about Ruby's marriage and child was a lie," I added. "Those could not have been motives for her death."

She nodded. "I got so scared when you said you'd overheard us. I didn't know how much you'd heard. It was so foolish to talk about stuff like that by an open window, but Ruby wanted to have a smoke. So I had to tell you something to explain why Ruby had met Lance and given him the brooch."

"I knew you were not being truthful with me," I said. "Your story did not explain the fear and pleading I'd heard in your voice. Why do you think Lance never contacted you after the war?"

"I don't know. I've wondered the same thing," Daphne said.

"Was he afraid of somebody back in America?" I asked, thinking back to the conversation I'd had with Mr. Lancaster at the Canterbury tearoom.

"I don't know," she whispered.

We stood in silence for a while. Suddenly, something occurred to me. "Why did you cancel your engagement on the morning of the announcement?" I asked.

"I panicked," she said. "I could not go through with it. It's against the law to marry someone while you are still married to somebody else."

"But why did you then agree to marry James?" I asked.

"By then I had heard that a journalist had been found by the gates. I knew it had to be Lance. I was free to marry, since this time he was really dead. And my mother was begging me to do it for the sake of my father's career. I have to marry someone, I suppose. So I agreed." She shrugged.

Why did that someone have to be James? I mused, crestfallen.

CHAPTER 27

A knock on the door brought us back to the present. "Daphne," came the voice and then the head of her father. "I heard some commotion earlier, and would have come sooner, but your mother was having trouble closing her trunk, and the servants weren't strong enough, so I had to sit on top of it..."

Seeing the distressed look on his daughter's face, he pushed into the room. "What is it, darling?"

Daphne began sobbing again.

"What is going on here?" he asked, looking between me and Daphne. "What are you doing to my daughter?" he growled, addressing me.

Mr. Carter walked up to his daughter and caressed her gently.

"Daddy," she sobbed into his chest. "Oh, Daddy, what am I supposed to do?"

"Shh, it's okay, pumpkin. It's alright." He patted her head. "Daddy will take care of it. I always take care of my little princess."

I gasped and jumped off the bed. "You killed

Lance and Ruby?" I asked, startled.

Of course, it all made sense now. He was the man Lance had been afraid of back in America. Mr. Carter was the reason Lance could not go back or contact Daphne.

He turned towards me, a deep scowl deforming his broad face. "What?"

As he was blocking my route to the door, I took a step towards the windows. I took a furtive glance. If need be, I could jump out and into the waiting bushes below. I would probably get away with just something broken.

"No! Of course I did not kill them! Well, I could have killed the swine, but he escaped to Europe," he snarled.

He hugged his daughter tighter. "You should have been honest with me, Daphne. I knew all about it. Since the very beginning."

"What?" Daphne sputtered. "How?"

"Ruby told me. She came to me after the marriage had taken place. She was scared. Lance had knifed Stan in a bar brawl. You see, Stan had got cold feet after your wedding. He was worried that I'd find out about it and that I'd be angry about his involvement in it. He thought it would be better to tell me. Lance and Stan argued. Lance knifed him and then enlisted in order to evade the police."

"Why didn't he contact Daphne after he left?" I asked.

"I threatened him, ordering him never to come back to the States and never to contact my daughter. I took care of the stabbing with the police. But if he ever disobeyed me, I would hand him over to the police."

Daphne's sobs had turned into full-blown wails.

"Shh, pumpkin," he patted her head.

"But if you knew about the marriage, how could you make your daughter marry someone else?" I asked. "It's bigamy, and it's illegal. Even if the marriage had taken place in a different country."

"I had lawyers working on it," Mr. Carter said. "Seven years had passed since he'd disappeared on her. After seven years with no contact, you can declare the deadbeat husband dead and annul the marriage." He returned his attention to his daughter. "I had taken care of everything, pumpkin."

"I didn't know," she said between sobs. "He began blackmailing me, daddy. It started when we arrived in England. Ruby met with him to pay him off. We didn't know you were working on the annulment...And why didn't she tell me you knew..."

"Ah, that's just the kind of kid she was," Mr. Carter said. "Always so loyal. I'd asked her not to tell you that I knew, in case you thought I was interfering in your life."

Mr. Carter was silent for a while.

"You and Ruby should have come to me and told me the truth," he said in a stern voice. "I didn't know the louse was blackmailing you. I didn't even know he was here until I heard someone had knocked him on the head. Good riddance." He released his daughter and began pacing the room. "The swine probably came after you because he knew you'd be too scared to tell me about it." He let out a robust sigh.

"But if you didn't kill him," I said, "then who did?"

"I'm sure he made enough enemies here as well," Mr. Carter answered. "Someone here killed him. It's got nothing to do with my family."

"What about Ruby?" I pressed.

"Ah, she just drowned, poor kid." Mr. Carter sighed again. "She was a good kid, but drank too much. She was an accident waiting to happen."

While Mr. Carter had been speaking, I had moved towards the windows and was gazing out on the gardens below, wondering who could have killed the journalist. And then I noticed the view out of Daphne's windows. From here, one could clearly see the path running along the edge of the woods.

"Daphne," I turned to her, "did you see James along that path, by the trees, on the day of the murder?" I pointed in its direction. "You were the one who told the police about seeing James walking back from where the body was discovered, weren't you?"

Daphne glanced from me to her father. "What if it was?" she countered with confidence, leaning a shoulder on her father's ample chest.

"But James is innocent," I said.

"I wouldn't be too sure about that, miss," Mr. Carter said. "Who else could it be? Lance probably had some dirt on him or his family. This Lord Haswell is as shady as they come."

I wondered for a moment what Mr. Carter meant, but Daphne interrupted my thoughts.

"I just wanted to go home," Daphne said. "I didn't want to marry James. Not really. I don't like England. And anyhow, what's the use of marrying him? I won't even get a title."

"So you denounced him to the police to get rid of him as a potential husband?!" I asked, outraged.

She just shrugged. Her eyes held no hint of remorse.

I stormed out of the room. I needed fresh air. If Daphne was not the killer—or her father—then who was?

I made my way down the grand staircase and towards the front doors.

Could Mrs. Carter be the killer? I considered. Her motives would have been the same as those of her husband and daughter. She had worked unrelentingly to arrange his marriage into the

British aristocracy. She'd even found a way to overcome Daphne's objections to Leopold, which, on reflection, were probably fabricated by Daphne as a ruse. Mrs. Carter would have been loath to let it all come to naught because of some meddling journalist. Even if he was Daphne's rightful husband.

As I walked out the front doors, I noticed the butler supervising a maid who was sweeping a spot on the front steps.

"One is glad that the American guests are leaving today, Lady Caroline," the butler said in a rare outburst of candor.

I smiled. "What's the matter?" I asked.

"The Americans have a habit of letting their cigarettes fall wherever they may. Once the ash gets worked into the stone, it's a troublesome stain to get out." He shook his head at the inconsiderate habit. "One here. One on the flagstones in front of the morning room—"

"The morning room?" I asked. The butler's remark had caught my attention. "Who has been leaving these cigarette stains?"

"One doesn't like to name names," the butler began, "but since they are leaving today...it's young Master Jack."

"Jack?!" I exclaimed. "Do you know where Jack is now?"

"He left not a minute ago. He asked to borrow one of Lord Haswell's automobiles. That's why he was standing on the stairs here, smoking. He was getting quite impatient as the chauffeur took quite some time to bring the car round."

"And do you know where he was heading?"

"He mentioned something about Croydon," the butler offered.

Jake had done a runner! And he was heading for a flight out of Croydon airport. "I need my car," I said. "Immediately."

"Yes, Your Ladyship."

I buzzed off down the drive as soon as my car arrived. Thankfully, it had only taken a minute.

As I drove down the driveway, and down the road towards the village, I could see dust in the distance, where Jack had passed. Fortunately, it had not rained in quite a while. If I drove fast enough, I might catch up with him.

I pressed the gas pedal and shifted gears.

At the crossroads, I hesitated for an instant. If Jack had been going to London, he would have turned left. But something about the dust hanging in the still air told me he had taken a turn towards Canterbury.

I swung my roadster in the direction of Canterbury, hoping I'd made the right decision. Crossing the river and the stone gates, I entered High Street.

Ahead, I heard a honk, the screech of tires, and then the crunch of metal on ancient stone.

CHAPTER 28

Just ahead, I saw Jack climbing out of the car he'd crashed into the stone walls surrounding the Precincts.

For a moment I wondered at the cause, and then the wispy hair, followed by the balding head of the vicar, popped up over the car's bonnet. He was picking up his brown parcels off the road. His Homburg had rolled down the road.

"Ah, Lady Caroline!" the vicar exclaimed. "You've remembered! I thought you had quite forgotten that today was the last day of the colloquium and we were meant to pick up our articles from the Deanery. And then, when I did not see you at breakfast, I resolved to make my own way here. It's quite a pleasant walk through the fields. But I must say, I'm glad you've arrived."

I smiled at the vicar. I had quite forgotten about him and his wares.

But while the vicar had been talking, I had not let Jack out of my sight. He was now leaning on the side of the car, lighting up a cigarette.

"Driving on the wrong side of the road is such a nuisance," Jack was saying to no one in particular. "And then this fool jumped right in front of the car." He gestured towards the vicar.

"I tripped. And spilled my packages. And then my hat blew off," the vicar said apologetically.

"No matter, vicar," I said. "You've done well. Now, if you don't mind, please deposit the packages in my car, and ask Louisa to fetch the police."

By this time, a crowd had gathered around us, and I knew Jack would have a hard time running away. I moved closer to him so we would not be overheard. Or at least not much.

"I thought you were headed to Croydon," I said.

"Is this not the way?" he asked, confused.

I shook my head. "You were doing a runner, weren't you? Perhaps trying to catch a flight to Paris? And then what? Were you planning to make your way to Africa? The steamer from Southampton was not departing soon enough for you? You couldn't wait to leave with your family?"

"What? What are you talking about?" He gazed at me with feigned disinterest.

"I know you killed Lance Bradford and Ruby. And I know why," I said. I was fairly certain I was right.

He just laughed. "I don't know what you are talking about. I was just on my way to see a buddy in Croydon. After my meeting, I was going to bring the car back to Lord Haswell."

I ignored his weak explanation. "You knew about your sister's marriage to Lance," I pressed.

He flinched slightly.

"You admitted to sneaking around to follow your sister. Did you follow her one day to the Clerk's office in New York, perhaps?"

He did not reply.

"I thought you were in love with Ruby, and that's why you watched her so closely and hung on her every word."

He laughed derisively.

I continued, unperturbed. "But you were worried that she would reveal Daphne's marriage to Lance when she was drunk. Once you had killed Lance, you had to do away with Ruby as well. She could not be trusted to keep a secret when she was drunk."

"And why would I do that? Who Daphne is or isn't married to makes no difference to me," he said.

"Oh, but I think it does," I countered. "You're an ambitious young man. You've worked hard to distance yourself from your family's humble beginnings—Princeton University, prestigious student societies. You cared who your sister married as much as the rest of your family. A marriage into the British aristocracy would have been a boon for your future political career. You couldn't let Lance or Ruby jeopardize that." My thoughts flitted to a moment after our tennis game. "You were worried that the wedding would be canceled," I added.

He flicked his cigarette away and glared at me.

"And another thing," I said, glancing at where his cigarette had fallen. "You knew James was going to meet with Lance by the gates. You overheard James and Leopold discussing the meeting while you were standing outside the morning room, smoking." I glared back at him.

"All this is circumstantial," he scoffed. "It would never stand up in court."

"So is the evidence against James," I said. "And he has no motive for killing neither the journalist nor Ruby."

He crossed his arms but did not relent. He was still leaning nonchalantly against the car, as though he had not a care in the world.

"My uncle saw you," I fibbed. "He saw you walking there and back. He can put you at the scene of the crime at the right time."

He smirked. "What?! That loony walking around the gardens in his gown?" He let out a laugh. "No one is going to believe him."

"He may look a bit odd," I said, trying to contain my rage, "but he is a peer of the realm. A lord. And in this country, his word carries more weight than yours," I said, scowling at him.

I wasn't entirely certain that my statement was true, but enamored as Jack was with the power offered by titles, I expected he would not know that.

Just then, a police siren pierced the air.

CHAPTER 29

"Ahoy, there!" Poppy bellowed at us from her sailboat. She clipped Leopold on the back to congratulate him on having overtaken our boat.

James and I were not racing against them, but with Poppy, everything was a competition.

It was another sunny day in Kent, with plenty of sea breeze to fill our sails. The beach of Hythe, where we'd have a picnic, was just visible in the distance. I waved heartily in return.

It was a few days after Jack had been arrested. And all charges against James had been dropped.

I could not be certain if a jury would find Jack guilty of Lance Bradford's murder. As Jack had so correctly observed, all the evidence against him was circumstantial. But perhaps, now that the police were on the right track, they would find more evidence against him.

Sadly, Ruby's death would probably remain in the official records as an accidental drowning.

The Carters had departed Resington Hall in disgrace. And in their wake followed the two American agents on a brass-rubbing holiday.

But all was not lost for Lady Haswell's cause to marry off Leopold.

"Your mother appears to be coming round to the idea of Poppy and Leopold," I said to James.

"Yes, Poppy possesses the attributes my mother has always praised most in a potential bride for Leopold—money and a willingness to overlook his shortcomings."

"Do you think they'll be happy together?" I asked, turning to James.

"Of course. If that's what Poppy tells Leopold to be," James said and smiled.

I laughed. It reminded me of something Poppy had said to me when I had asked her about her feelings for Leopold: "I think he was jolly well taken with me when I told him that he was holding his binoculars quite wrong."

To the casual observer, Poppy and Leopold formed an ill-matched couple, both in physique and temperament. But I was quite convinced that they were perfectly suited to each other.

Although overbearing, Poppy thrived in the role of a leader. She would inspect, catalog and oversee every part of Leopold's life, and encourage him, boisterously, to his highest potential. And Leopold's reticent character would certainly benefit from the unyielding support she would offer even to his most eccentric interests.

James and I sailed further on, the pleasant breeze cooling our sun-warmed skin. I breathed in the fresh sea air.

My thoughts fleeted to the events of the past few days, and I wanted to ask James if he would have gone through with his betrothal to Daphne, but some questions were better left a mystery.

"You know, it was your mother who suggested an American bride for Leopold," James interrupted my thoughts. "She recommended an advertisement in *The Titled American*."

"Really?" I said. I wondered at my mother's intent.

"And rumor has it that it was she who arranged Cecil's engagement," James added.

I stared at him in disbelief. What was he implying? Was it possible that I'd been mistaken about my mother all this time? No, I shook my head, I had a collection of telegrams that proved otherwise.

But perhaps she had been as little keen on Cecil and Leopold as I had been.

I glanced at James. He smiled at me, and his blue eyes sparkled in the summer's sunshine, while the breeze tousled the golden waves of his hair.

After a few moments, during which I'd tried to reconcile this newfound knowledge about my mother with what I knew of her, he said: "My mother didn't want you at Leopold's engagement party."

The revelation surprised me and yet it

explained her uncharitable looks towards me. "Lady Haswell was against my coming?! But why?"

"Did you not notice how few girls were invited?" James asked instead of answering my question.

I nodded. I had noticed something to that effect.

"This was by design. My mother didn't want anyone impeding Leopold's chance of success this time. And since Leopold had proposed to you numerous times, she was worried that he would not go through the engagement if you were there to distract him."

"He never really had any serious intentions towards me," I said. "I doubt he ever really liked me. He was only doing what he was told by your mother. I would have made him miserable."

"No, you're right. I don't think he would have appreciated you," James said, and threw me a quick sidelong glance.

I turned away to hide my smile. I wanted to ask him what he appreciated about me, but a wave of shyness caught me off-guard and prevented me from speaking. Since sharing a terribly exciting kiss, I now somehow felt bashful in James' company.

I mused, discombobulated by the thought, that the shared intimacy, instead of abating my fears, had made me feel more self-conscious around James. What he said, the way he looked at me, and what he thought of me became even more paramount.

"So why did Lady Haswell invite me in the end?" I asked timidly.

"Because I'd asked her to," James answered with confidence.

A warmth, completely unconnected to the August sun, melted through my body.

"What about Poppy?" I asked, trying to mask the blush I was certain was blossoming on my cheeks. "Why was she the only other young woman invited?"

"She was the one girl my mother considered safe enough," he replied.

We both laughed at the irony.

"Caroline," he began, "you know we can't take away from their spotlight. Not until after their wedding. Leopold doesn't get many opportunities to shine."

I smiled and nodded. I understood.

After his release, James and I had come to an understanding. But now was not the moment to let our parents, or even our friends, know. The next few months would be busy with preparations for Poppy and Leopold's engagement and then their wedding.

"And what about Resington Hall?" I asked. "Your father is unlikely to find such a willing buyer for it anytime soon."

"Oh, the most curious thing occurred. My father received a letter from a Hollywood producer. He had seen a photograph of the house in an article about Ruby's death. The producer wants to use it for an upcoming movie about Dracula."

As I drove back home, with the vicar by my side, I let my mind wander over all the events that had transpired. And I considered that I was awfully glad my father's cross had not been discovered at Resington Hall. It would have been a terrible nuisance. There would have been a great deal of justification and elucidation required on all sides.

I found Father sitting in his study, staring at his desk, a few hours after I had arrived back from Kent.

"I heard you found your cross," I said, the surprise evident in my voice. "Had you misplaced it?" I asked and kissed him on the head like a small child.

"It's the most extraordinary thing," he said, sounding bewildered. "I could have sworn I looked in this drawer several times." He opened and closed the said drawer a few more times for good measure, as though the mystery would reveal itself.

I kissed him one more time, on the cheek, and left him to ponder the mysteries of life, while I exited through his study doors into the garden.

Birds sang, bumblebees buzzed, and my heart was light. I entered the rose garden and touched the flower heads as I walked by. The perfume of their fragrant oil filled the warm summer air.

In the seclusion of the walled garden, I pondered my subterfuge.

For I had been carrying the cross of the Order of the Conqueror's Companions with me all this time. It was I who took it from my father's study.

I had no malicious intent. I simply wanted to go to the engagement party.

I'd known about the Haswells' financial difficulties, about their visit to our house, and about Lord Haswell's rivalry with my father. And having an inkling of how my mother would react to the engagement party invitation, I'd swiped the cross on the morning the invitation arrived.

Taking the cross and suggesting that one of my parent's visitors had pilfered it had been my plan to preempt my mother.

I made my way through the gardens and entered the drawing room where my mother was sitting under her Sargent portrait. It appeared that the cat and she had reached a resolution to their impasse. The cat was sitting in my mother's lap.

"Ah, Caroline. You're back!" my mother exclaimed upon my entrance. "Wait till you hear the latest news! Lady Morton has just written to inform me that her dear Cecil is no longer engaged."

I gazed at my mother with interest. If James' estimations of my mother were correct, she was just taunting me for sport and had no intention of saddling me with Cecil.

But I was far safer away from England.

I wondered where Uncle Albert would travel next.

THE END

Thank you for reading *Trouble on a Country Lane*,
Book 4 in the Lady Caroline Murder Mysteries series.
The adventures continue in Book 5, *Secret of the Scarab*,
a trip of murder and mayhem, with the odd beetle or two thrown in, through Egypt.

Secret of the Scarab
(Book 5 of the Lady Caroline Murder Mysteries)

Leave it to Lady Caroline and Uncle Albert to inadvertently stumble upon an ancient load of trouble in Egypt. Ancient curses, lost treasure and murder... the way only Lady Caroline and Uncle Albert can do it!

One of my favorite parts about writing historical mysteries is the research. Visit https://isabellabassett.com if you would like to read the **Historical Notes** for this book, or any of the other books in the Lady Caroline series.

On my website, you can also get in touch with me, sign up for email, learn more about this and other mystery series I write, or to read about beautiful Switzerland, where I live.

MORE BOOKS BY ISABELLA BASSETT

The Old Bookstore Mysteries series about an old Swiss bookstore with a peculiar black cat.

Book 1: Out of Print

Book 2: Murderous Misprint

Book 3: Suspicious Small Print

Book 4: Reckless Reprint

Book 5: Incriminating Imprint

Book 6: Scandalous Snow Print

Book 7: Blackmail Blueprint

Printed in Great Britain
by Amazon